I0461598

WHEAT

By

FRED DOUGHTY

WHEAT

Copyright © 2012 CELTIC AMERICA BOOKS

All rights reserved.

ISBN:0985303018
ISBN-13:978-0985303013

This Book Is Dedicated to

Amy Irene "Rosebud" Atchinson
&
Collin Russell Doughty

"Only A Matter Of Time.."

WHEAT

CHAPTERS

WHEAT

ACKNOWLEDGMENTS

Irene Doughty and the Delphi and Black Lake Family

Mary Sceva

Robert & Louise Collins

Sam Patrick at Digital 1 Media

Don Jenkins at Musical Concept's Studio B

And of course...Linda

WHEAT

*To everything there is a season, and a time to every purpose under the heaven;
a time to be born, and a time to die...*

WELCOME TO WHEAT

Prelude

Wheat wasn't much different than any other small town in the southeast corner of Kansas. In fact, if it weren't for the welcome signs posted along the road just outside of town you'd never know it was there. A few scattered old and weathered dried up red brick buildings with a road running through the middle. It was somewhere that was nowhere and if you weren't paying close attention you would never know you'd been there.

1n 1948 the opening of U.S. Route 75, built ten miles to the west, was the scorcher that dried up what little business there was left in Wheat. Until then, Kinney's Gasoline and Automobile Repair, Parsons Hardware & Feed, Margie's Diner, the Dixon County Building, and a couple other small businesses had been holding their own. Wheat had been a handy stop for traveling folks once upon a time. It was nestled between the growing city of Independence to the south and Topeka, the state capital to the north. Wheat was rarely mentioned on most maps. At least that is the way it was before the little town made big news. The trouble is it wasn't good news. It started with the mysterious and bloody killing of local man, Ernie Parsons, and it ended with one of the most bizarre murder trials in the history of Kansas.

Some folks say that the death of Ernie Parsons was so horrible that the governor intentionally constructed U.S. Route 75 a good distance around Wheat to keep people from going near there. Eventually, Wheat's gruesome reputation would disappear over time. But unfortunately, like the paint fading away on its dried up walls so did the little town of Wheat.

The witnesses of this old story are long gone now, all but me. I was only ten years old at the time but I remember the story well. It is me that keeps the story alive.

A STRANGER ARRIVES IN TOWN
Chapter One

Margie Kittles was the first soul in Wheat to meet the quiet stranger. He didn't have a name then. He was just a visitor or maybe someone who had lost his way that wandered into town one summer day. It was early July in 1933 and there had been a long spell without rain. The man was alone and walked into Margie's Diner at 6:00 a.m. sharp, just as Margie was hanging up the open sign in the restaurant's front window. Wearing a clean white cotton suit with a short, wide, red and blue silk tie, the quiet stranger walked in and sat by a window in a booth seat. He looked to be in his early forties but had one of those faces that made it hard to guess.

"Good morning, can I get you some coffee to start you out?" Margie called out as she put on her apron behind the counter.

The man said nothing and folded his hands on the table, simply smiling as he looked around the room. Margie assumed that her first customer of the day hadn't heard her and poured him a cup anyway.

"Cream or sugar?" she asked as she sat the cup on the table in front of him. The man who had been looking out the window snapped to attention and gave Margie a big grateful smile. Margie waited for his answer, but after a long empty pause she told him, "Well, if you want any just let me know."

Pointing to a chalkboard behind the counter Margie told the lone customer, "Fresh ham today, Friday Special. Three eggs, anyway you like 'em, a thick slice of ham, taters, and a biscuit for six bits, includes your coffee. Menu is there on the table if you'd like something else."

The man just pleasantly smiled without saying anything.

Margie smiled back for a moment with a puzzled look on her face and then finally added, "You take your time, just let me know when you're ready, hon." She walked back behind the counter to get ready for another slow day.

Pete Barnes was one of Margie's best customers and was her second patron of the day. He was a widower and owned 640 acres of prime farmland just outside of Wheat, half of which was handed down to him from his father who had been a homesteader. Pete did pretty well for himself as did a few other farmers in the region. Like every farmer in southeast Kansas, Pete wore the same worn out overalls every day, except Sunday, when he put on his clean ones. The tradition of wearing "Sunday's best" was just good manners and what every respectable Kansas man ought to do.

"Mornin' Margie," Pete said with the same cheery voice he had nearly every morning for close to twenty years.

"Mornin Pete, comin' right up," Margie answered. Hotcakes and coffee had been Pete Barnes' Friday breakfast through the years. The lean man with the weathered skin gave a friendly nod to the stranger as he made his way to his favorite counter stool. The stranger smiled back and sipped on his cup of coffee.

"Say, how 'bout that, I beat Big Tom this morning," Pete bragged to Margie as she flipped his hotcakes. Big Tom Kinney, the owner of the town's only gasoline filling station, was usually the first one to arrive for breakfast, especially on Fridays. Big Tom spent nearly a full day's earnings for breakfast on Fridays. It was his one big treat and at nearly 300 pounds he would generally put away three of Margie's Friday Specials.

Margie looked over her shoulder, "It's not like Big Tom to sleep in," she replied. "He didn't look so good yesterday, kinda grey. Not much of an appetite either."

"I can't imagine Tom with no appetite," Pete joked. "He'd put you out of business."

Margie chuckled in agreement as she stacked the pancakes on a plate and poured Pete a cup of coffee. Pete motioned with his eyes asking silently who the stranger was. Margie shrugged her shoulders and raised her eye brows indicating that she didn't know.

She then called out to the stranger, "You ready to order, hon?" The man seemed totally distracted as he looked out the window and didn't answer. Margie and Pete looked at each other perplexed. "Mister?" Margie called out. There was no response. Margie stepped out from behind the counter and walked over to the stranger's table. Pete watched from his stool as he took a drink of coffee.

"Mister, are you okay?" Margie asked with concern. The stranger finally noticed the woman leaning towards him and he smiled back at her. "I'll be," Margie said aloud, "I believe this man is deaf." Taking a pencil that was propped behind her ear, Margie pulled out a receipt and wrote on the back, *"What would you like for breakfast?"* She placed it on the table in front of the man and he picked it up and looked at it. He then looked at Margie and only smiled. "Well, how do you like that, he can't read either, poor dear."

"Get him your Special, I'm buying," Pete told her.

Margie smiled back at the stranger and patted him on his shoulder. He seemed perfectly harmless and was sort of a handsome man with his thick head of black hair and honest eyes. She returned behind the counter and looked curiously at the stranger. "I wonder where he came from?" she asked. "Did you see his automobile out there?"

"Nope," Pete replied, "only rig out there is my truck. He must have got himself a ride here from somewhere. Wonder where he's trying to get to?"

Margie shook her head, "Boy, I don't know, but he must have taken a wrong turn to end up in this old dust bowl. Want more coffee?"

Sheriff Dan Devine came through the door, removed his hat, gave the stranger a quick look-over and a howdy-nod and sat on a stool beside Peter Barnes. "Mornin' folks," he said with a tired flat tone.

"You look like hell, Dan," Pete told him, "you have a long night?"

The sheriff placed his hat on the counter top next to him and delivered the bad news, "Long mornin', Big Tom died sometime last night." Pete and Margie's mouth dropped open with shock.

"Never came home after work yesterday," the sheriff continued, "his wife thought he had gone out for a beer down in Independence. When he didn't come home she called me up. I found him lying on the floor of his filling station this morning around 3 o'clock, dead and cold."

Margie's eyes began to fill with tears. "What happened to him?"

"Heart gave out, I suppose," the sheriff answered. "I had to wake up Ernie Parsons and Skinny Jim Carter to help me load him up in my truck. Took him home, his wife wanted him there. The coroner from Montgomery County is going to come out later today and pick up the body since our own coroner run off with that Mexican girlfriend of his last spring."

Pete Barnes shook his head. "That's a shame. I don't like to sound mean-hearted but that man was no trophy."

The sheriff and Margie looked at Pete with a mixture of surprise and disgust.

Pete noticed the way they were looking at him and put down his coffee cup. "I'm not talking about Big Tom, I'm talking about that so-called coroner. That coroner, Sam what's-his-name, looked like one of his clients."

"How's Big Tom's wife taking it, Dan?" Margie asked.

"Like any other mother of five kids with no daddy. I don't know how they're going to get by," the sheriff answered, "they got nothing here."

"Big Tom's got family down in Independence," Pete added, "I think she's from Wichita. I'm sure they will be all right."

"Well I'm going out there and take them some food and see what we all can do," Margie insisted. "Big Tom Kinney was always there for everyone in this town and we need to do right and help out his family."

Both men agreed.

"Keep me posted, Margie," Pete said, "I'll do what I can. And let her know that I am very sorry for her loss."

Margie pulled up a long strand of hair that had fallen from the top of her head and clipped it back into place. "My goodness, I need to get breakfast going for that poor man."

"Who's our visitor?" the sheriff asked quietly. "Didn't see any extra rigs out front."

"He can't hear ya," Pete answered, "he's as deaf as a telephone pole. Don't seem to be able to talk neither, nor read."

"Who is he?" the sheriff asked as he turned to look at the stranger. "Where'd he come from?"

The quiet stranger looked at the three people who were staring at him and smiled back at them.

"Your guess is as good as ours, Dan." Margie answered. "Seems plenty nice though."

The sheriff took a final sip of his coffee and commented, "So does a wolverine until it bites ya." The sheriff slapped down a dime on the counter and headed for the door. "I got to get some sleep. I'll talk to you two later."

Margie watched the sheriff walk out the door passing Ed Morlan, a local retired teacher, who was just walking in. Sheriff Devine politely held the door open as Ed gave him a grateful grin, "Mornin' Sheriff, thank you."

"Good morning Ed," the sheriff replied and tipped the brim of his hat.

Ed Morlan stepped in and walked over to a wall where he placed his jacket and hat on a hook. He headed towards the counter and glanced over at the stranger who was carefully watching him. Ed smiled and the stranger smiled back. The two kept their eyes on each other until Ed took a stool at the counter.

"Good morning, handsome," Margie told him as she poured a cup of coffee and placed it on the counter in front of him. Ed raised his eye brows and sat down slowly. He was a short man, 77 years old with round wire framed glasses with lenses so thick his eyes looked enormous.

Ed's eyes lightened up and replied, "Hey good lookin', where you been all my life?"

Margie looked over her shoulder as she worked at the grill, "Ed, my dear man, I have been right here this whole time. I've been waiting for you to come by and take me away."

Pete Barnes cut in, "Excuse me but would you two like to be alone?"

Margie giggled, "Ed, you know if I had a mind to, you and I would run off to New York City right now."

"Yup," Ed replied. "We'd be puttin' on the Ritz, eh Margie?"

"You betcha," Margie answered. "You gonna have the Special, sugar?"

"Nope," Ed told her, "Cream of Wheat cause I'm training for the Olympics. I'm going for the gold. Boxing, heavy weight division this time, think I got a chance?"

"Go for it, Ed," Margie told him, "I think you could even beat Jesse Owens."

"He's a runner," Ed corrected her. "I just want to go over there and pop that Adolf Hitler in the chops."

"Oh, is he a pretty good boxer?" asked Margie.

Pete Barnes chimed in, "I think he's the German president or something."

"He's a *nut* is what he is," Ed told them. "Could you throw some honey on that Cream of Wheat, Margie?"

"Sure thing, hon." Margie answered.

Margie turned around and walked up to the counter in front of Ed Morlan. Lowering her voice she asked him, "Ed, honey, did you hear about Big Tom, Big Tom Kinney?" Ed perked up with interest and shook his head. "He's dead," Margie informed him. "Died sometime during the night in his shop. Dan Devine found him there after his wife called when Big Tom didn't come home last night. Heart attack probably, but don't quote me on that."

Ed leaned forward, "You don't say. That is a shame." Ed sat up and looked as though he had remembered something. Turning around in his stool he looked over at the stranger sitting quietly at the window seat obviously not paying attention to what they were talking about.

Ed turned back to Margie and Pete and asked, "When did Dan find the body?"

"Round three this morning," Pete answered, "his body was cold when Dan found him."

Ed appeared as though he was thinking hard about something and said, "Interesting."

Margie tilted her head, "Why do you say that, Ed?"

"Oh, probably nothing," Ed told her as he took another drink of coffee, "just thinking to myself."

But Ed Morlan had remembered something, maybe just a coincidence so he kept this thoughts to himself. He turned his head to look at the stranger who looked back at him with a friendly smile. The stranger remained still and totally quiet as if he was oblivious to where he was, he did look pleasant though and perfectly content.

SUMMER CHORES
Chapter Two

Hazel Spragg inherited her sizeable old house from her parents who died ten years earlier and was in need of a new wood stove. Over at Ernie Parsons Hardware & Feed, Millie Parsons was going through the new Montgomery-Wards catalogue with Hazel. The "Chester King" model looked to be the best selection and had a fair price at $68.50. "You are probably looking at four to six weeks for delivery," Millie told her customer and long time friend, "it will be coming all the way from Vermont."

At forty-nine years old Hazel was considered by some to be a spinster. Be that as it may, Miss Spragg's lack of a husband was not by choice. To say that she possessed a tall gaunt frame and a homely face was being kind. Hazel Spragg was far from being a good catch when it came to looks, but to kind hearted folks like Millie Parsons, Hazel was a sweet woman and terribly lonely.

"That will be just fine, Millie," Hazel replied, "just as long as I have it before October. I don't know how I'm going to get it over to the house and hook it all up though."

Millie closed the catalog and pushed it to the side. "You don't worry about that Hazel, Ernie will take care of it. He's got plenty of energy and more than enough time." Millie looked upward towards the roof where the sounds of busy hammering and sawing were taking place.

13

Ernie Parsons was atop a tall ladder that he had leaned against the front porch of the Hardware & Feed and was banging on a long piece of sheet metal with a ball-peen hammer. Ernie was a big man, built rugged, and worked fast and furious on every task he took on. He was stubborn and didn't have much patience for any job that required it. He was one who would force something to work whether it wanted to cooperate or not. Nothing came easy to Ernie Parsons.

Ernie and Millie Parsons moved to Wheat in the spring of 1919 and started up Parsons Hardware & Feed. They chose the town of Wheat for two reasons; one reason was Dixon County had no hardware or farm supplies to offer at the time and folks had to run all the way down to Independence in Montgomery County, which was a good distance away. The other reason wasn't so obvious, at least to most folks. Ernie Parsons had joined the battle in France in 1917 and was sent home after only two weeks of fighting. The army doctors told him that his nerves had been jarred badly from all the shelling that his platoon had taken and he wasn't useful to the cause anymore. Ernie was bitter about being sent home, but his faithful wife Millie was mightily relieved. However, the Ernie that had left to fight the Germans wasn't the same Ernie who came home. He was irritable and sometimes just plain mean. Millie loved her man though and was kind and patient with him. The two were unable to have children and worked hard at their business to make ends meet.

Willy McCabe enjoyed spending his summer days over at Parsons Hardware & Feed helping out. His dad was a road salesman and almost always worked out of town. His mom, Ruthie, was generally busy raising Willy's two year old little sister. Sitting around the house all day was mighty boring to a kid with a big imagination and he was happy to socialize with anyone who would pay attention to him. There were always lots of things to do and people to see at the hardware & feed store. Willy never got in the way and was actually quite useful at times, loading bags of seed and fertilizer onto trucks and wagons and helping with other things whenever needed. Ernie Parsons wasn't much of a conversationalist but he certainly was interesting enough. Millie Parsons showed her appreciation by frequently rewarding the boy with homemade treats for his efforts.

Down at the foot of the ladder ten year old Willy McCabe covered his eyes to block the sun as he looked up to watch and listen to Ernie Parsons working on his project. "Bring me up some more nails kid, 16's," Ernie ordered.

Willy jumped. He knew exactly what Ernie wanted, 16 penny nails. It was one of the many handy things that Willy had learned helping out at the Parsons Hardware & Feed. "Coming up!" Willy shouted as he ran to the porch and grabbed a handful of the galvanized nails from one of the boxes Ernie had brought out for his project. Carefully placing the nails in his shirt pocket Willy returned to the base of the ladder and looked up. Ernie was looking down at him motioning the boy with his hand to have him bring the nails up the ladder. It was a ways up and Willy was a bit fearful about the climb. He'd never been that high up on any ladder. In fact, he'd never been up a ladder.

Ernie Parsons looked back down and saw that Willy was still glued to the ground. "Come on boy, I need those nails," Ernie insisted.

Willy carefully began his ascent and told himself not to look down. Holding tightly to the ladder, sliding his hands on the rails, but never letting go, Willy slowly placed one foot on each step and concentrated on his every move. One step, two step, three and after what seemed an eternity, Willy was finally within reach of Ernie who saw that the nervous boy had a death grip on the ladder. Ernie held out his hand while Willy hooked his arm around the rail of the ladder clinging for dear life. With his free hand Willy carefully pulled out the nails from his shirt pocket and handed them to Ernie, not dropping one.

Now that Willy had conquered climbing the ladder he felt pretty good about himself. Looking around he could see things he hadn't noticed before. The second floor rooms of the county building had old furniture stacked up to the ceiling. Kinney's auto repair had three bald tires laying on its roof and a Red Rider wagon without any wheels. Margie's Diner looked smaller than it looked from the ground and there were small pipes poking out of the roof.

"Whatcha workin' on Ernie?" Willy asked.

Ernie was struggling and muttering to himself as he cut a piece of thin metal with a pair of metal snips. Wiping sweat from his brow with his sleeve Ernie told the boy, "Rain trough for the roof." Willy watched Ernie carefully handling and bending the thin metal wearing his thick leather gloves.

"Rain trough?" Willy replied. "Whatcha need that for? It don't rain around here much."

Ernie stopped doing what he was doing and looked down at Willy. "You sound like my wife, boy," Ernie said with frustration. "When it *does* rain we'll be ready."

Willy raised his eyebrows and thought about it. He then shook his head in agreement, "Yeah, I guess that does make sense, Ernie, I suppose."

Willy could almost always tell when someone was treating him like a little boy. He knew when he was being patronized by an adult simply to get him out of the way. Ernie was different though. He spoke his mind and although it wasn't always what Willy wanted to hear, at least Willy knew where he stood. Not many adult folks were so honest.

"Want some more nails, Ernie?" Willy asked.

"Nope," Ernie replied. Ernie snipped away at the end of a piece of metal.

"Boy, seems a lot hotter up here, huh Ernie?" Willy commented hoping for conversation.

"Yup," Ernie answered dryly without any more to offer.

"This would be a pretty neat place to make a fort, you gonna keep this ladder here?" Willy asked.

"Nope," Ernie quickly answered.

It was a pretty good day in Willy's world. He remained on the ladder the entire time Ernie Parsons worked on his rain trough project asking lots of questions that got lots of quick answers. Ernie Parsons didn't mind. In fact, besides his wife Millie, Willy McCabe was the only soul in Wheat that Ernie trusted.

THE WIDOW SWANSON
Chapter Three

Clara Swanson was eighty-four years old going on twenty-five. She had more energy and wit than any one person within two hundred miles in any direction. Having been the wife of a Presbyterian minister, Clara practiced her Christian faith daily and was known to be upright, trustworthy, and very religious. Wheat was her mission field, but as the Lord would have it, Clara had to sow those seeds of faith alone since her husband fell dead at the pulpit in 1929 during a lecture up in Wichita. Since then Clara was dubbed with the lonely title, "Widow Swanson."

Widow Swanson was a helpful contributor to the community. She raised chickens and supplied eggs to anyone who wanted them at no cost. Her garden was well managed and she was always good to lend a dollar or two if someone had a need. "Pay me back when you can but not until then," she would say with a sweet and sincere voice.

But not everyone looked forward to seeing the Widow Swanson coming their way. There were some days when folks just didn't want to hear "The Lord this" and "The Lord that." The Widow Swanson never really preached at you, she just made it very clear that when things weren't going right, it was because of the lack of God Almighty in your life. Folks who didn't want to get *religious* knew better than to complain about anything to the Widow Swanson.

Wheat was the county seat in Dixon County, in fact, Wheat was the only town in the county. Everyone got along fairly well mainly because they had to. Times were tough and any helping hand in an emergency was your closest neighbor. Skinny Jim Carter had to have his dislocated elbow reset by Ed Morlan one time after falling off the back of his tractor. A long bumpy ride to the hospital all the way down to Independence would have been very painful.

It was on a Saturday around 2:00 p.m. when Clara Swanson met the quiet stranger for the first time. He was with Margie Kittles leaving the diner after closing up early for the day.

"Hello Margie," Clara called from across the street. Clara Swanson had come in to town to buy a sympathy card for Big Tom Kinney's wife. The 10-Cent Store next to the Dixon County Building was small but had a little bit of everything, including gift cards. Big Tom's grave-side service was planned for Sunday afternoon at the old Wheat Cemetery on the northeast side of town at three o'clock. The Widow Swanson had volunteered to supply most of the food for the gathering that would take place at the Kinney's home after the funeral. Clara Swanson was pleased to have the opportunity to demonstrate her Christian witness, "love thy neighbor" and such.

"Hi Clara," Margie waved back as she walked towards her truck that was parked beside the diner. The quiet stranger who was walking behind Margie stopped, looked over at Clara, smiled, and then waved as well. Clara Swanson's curiosity got the best of her. She walked across the street hoping to ignite a conversation with Margie to find out who the visitor was.

"Calling it a day, Margie?" Clara asked. Margie rested one hand on her hip and with the other hand pulled back a strand of hair that was always falling in her face.

"Yep, I got a lot of things to do before Big Tom's service. Got to clean up some folding chairs and load up a couple of folding tables at the house to take over there tomorrow. Sure is going to be strange not having Big Tom around anymore."

Clara nodded her head in sympathetic agreement. "He is certainly going to be missed, especially by that family of his. We'll need to all pull together for Betty and those kids, take them all under our wings." Clara said.

Margie noticed Clara Swanson's eyes spending a good amount of the time looking at the man standing quietly beside her. "Oh, I'm sorry Clara, this is…well, he's new in town, came here yesterday morning. He can't hear a thing we're saying and doesn't speak a word. He'll be staying at Skinny Jim Carter's for a spell until we can figure out who he is and where he's going."

Clara was surprised and her face showed it. "How odd," she thought to herself. Things like this didn't happen in Wheat. Clara offered her hand to the man who received it and shook it politely with a smile. "What's his name?" Clara asked.

"Don't have any idea," Margie answered, "nobody knows anything about him. He seems to be a nice man though and he is very helpful. He spent the day with me yesterday and again today cleaning up around the diner and washing up dishes. And he helped Skinny Jim last night painting screen doors. Very helpful."

"My goodness," Clara Swanson commented. "Well, I hope he finds his way to where he's going. And I hope his family isn't somewhere worrying about him." Clara was very suspicious. The scriptures warned of wolves in sheep clothing, but at the same time one must be kind to a stranger. Especially if the stranger was in need. "It was good to meet you, sir," Clara told the quiet man. "I should let you go Margie, we both have our hands full," Clara said as she broke away from the two. "I'll be seeing you tomorrow."

"We'll see you tomorrow, Clara," Margie said. "Oh by the way, if you're looking for a card for Big Tom's wife, good luck. All of their sympathy cards are bought up, nothing but old birthday and anniversary cards left."

"Oh, diddles," Clara said, "I guess I'll make her one by hand." As Clara walked back across the street towards the 10-Cent Store she looked back at Margie and the man walking behind her. He turned his head, smiled nicely and waved again at her. Clara was embarrassed and felt a little awkward at being caught looking back, but smiled and gave a quick wave before scooting on to her business.

The graveside service was short, partly because most everything had been said at the Wheat Good Shepherd Lutheran Chapel. But mostly it had gotten very hot and wearing black dresses and suits on a 95 degree day under the direct sun was not healthy even for a seasoned farmer. The entire town of Wheat and families from as far as Comanche County attended, fifty-five in all, including kids.

Afterwards the crowd met at the Kinney's home for eats and neighborly conversation. Big Tom's wife, Betty, was understandably not very talkative but showed her appreciation as best she could. Her five kids, two through eleven years old, laughed and played with the other children as if they were totally unaware of their missing daddy.

The quiet stranger sat in the backyard on a folding chair under the direct afternoon sun watching the children running and carrying on. Most everyone else hid in the shade on the back porch or under a large Tupelo tree sharing stories of Big Tom. Margie Kittles did her best at keeping everyone cooled down by filling their glasses full of sweetened lemon juice. Clara Swanson and Willy McCabe's mom, Ruthie, were preparing the food for all the guests.

Willy found his way to the kitchen following his nose to the alluring smells of the feast that was about ready to be eaten. There was ham, baked chicken, slow roasted beef, and lemon pies and more. "Wilbur Arthur McCabe, you get your fingers out of that cake," Ruthie snapped after catching her son swiping some frosting off of a chocolate cake. Willy jumped back and quickly stuck his chocolate covered finger in his mouth before his mother could grab it. "You need to get out there and visit, Willy, we will call you when it's time to eat," his mother scolded him.

"Who is that man out there, mom?" Willy asked.

"What man are you talking about? There are lots of men out there," she replied.

"The man in the white suit with the red and blue tie sitting all alone, who is he?" Willy asked.

"He's new in town," Clara Swanson informed the boy as she uncovered a pot of boiling corn. "Probably just passing through. Nobody really knows. It seems he's not able to hear or speak either, poor soul. Oh, diddles, this corn still isn't ready."

"Is that so?" Ruthie McCabe commented.

"That's what I've been told," Clara replied. "I met him briefly yesterday. Seems like a nice man. I hear he is very helpful."

"Can't speak either?" Willy asked with surprise in his voice.

"That's what I hear," Clara Swanson told him, "and we don't even know his name, kind of strange if you ask me."

Willy looked out at the man through a back window of the kitchen. This was exciting stuff. Nothing like this ever happens in Wheat, he thought. "For a man who can't hear or speak he sure seems happy," Willy said quietly while trying to imagine what it must be like not being able to hear or talk. The quiet man kicked a ball back to the kids playing near his chair and seemed to be having fun with the children.

"Zachariah!" Willy said with excitement in his voice.

"Who?" his mother asked.

"Zachariah," Willy repeated. "His name is Zachariah."

Willy's mom cut through a loaf of bread and shook her head, "What on earth are you talking about now, Willy?"

Clara Swanson smiled, "Zachariah was a priest, John the Baptist's father. God took Zachariah's voice for not believing a message that was sent to him." She was pleased that little Willy had remembered the biblical story.

"Well whoever he is you stay away from him," Ruthie warned her son. "He is still a stranger and you don't be talking to no strangers."

Willy walked back over to the table where the desserts were and looked closely at all the pies. He shrugged his shoulders, "He wouldn't hear me if I did talk to him, least that's what folks are sayin,"

"Don't be back-talking me young man," his mother snapped back.

Clara Swanson looked over at Willy and gave him a wink of an eye for support.

Out in the backyard the gathering of friends and family continued relaxing and chatting. The men folk naturally conversed with the men folk and the ladies with their kind. Most of the men had removed their suit coats and rolled up the sleeves of their white shirts. A light breeze kept the occasion bearable.

Many people were wondering who the quiet man was that was sitting alone, and Skinny Jim Carter was quick to inform them.

"Is he a relative of Big Tom's?" Lloyd Willis asked.

"No," Skinny Jim answered, "he just showed up a couple days ago and nobody knows who he is. He's been real helpful though, and he's a good worker. If you want to get something done you just have to show him and he seems to be happy as a clam doing it."

"Now that's the kind of help I can use around the farm," Ray Horne added, halfway joking. "I got three grown boys and they're all worthless."

Ed Morlan wasn't so sure. "There's something that just don't seem right," he said as he pulled off his thick glasses to wipe the sweat off his forehead. "Someone doesn't just drop out of the sky one day. I'm not too sure about this fellow."

"Well, send him my way when you're done with him, Jim," Tom Corbett butted in. "I could use some help digging a drainage ditch. I'll make it worth his while."

Ernie Parsons was nearby leaning against the trunk of the tree and keeping to himself while listening to the conversation about the quiet stranger. Ernie didn't take to new folks very well. "Kraut," Ernie spoke out as he filled his cheek with some Red Man tobacco.

Ray Horne turned around, "What was that Ernie?"

Ernie, looking a little disturbed, didn't say anything but kept his eyes on the stranger.

On the covered back porch a group of women including Millie Parsons and Hazel Spragg fanned themselves with Silver Screen magazines borrowed from Betty Kinney's house. Hazel was mesmerized by the nice looking man sitting alone at the edge of the yard and did her best at not making it obvious she was interested in him. The children had picked him out and were teasing him by kicking a ball near his chair. They shrieked in delight when he kicked it back their way.

"My, the children have found a friend to play with," Hazel mentioned.

Millie Parsons wondered when Hazel would finally bring the man up. "Yes, I noticed that. He seems to be genuinely enjoying them."

Hazel watched the man hoping to get eye contact with him. "Who is he?" she bravely asked.

"I don't know who he is," Millie replied, "I've never seen him before today."

"His name is Zachariah," Willy McCabe informed the women as he walked by them on his way to the backyard.

"Zachariah?" Hazel asked.

"Yep," Willy answered as he skipped away to play with the others.

From that moment on the quiet man had a name. It just as well could have been "Lester" or "Earl" or a hundred other regular names, but for now, for the folks in Wheat, he would be called Zachariah.

HENRY COYOTE
Chapter Four

It's been three weeks since Zachariah showed up in Wheat. He was becoming pretty popular with the locals and his reputation as being "real helpful" was growing. He did a fine job helping Tom Corbett dig a deep drainage ditch in hard ground that had more rocks than dirt. He also helped Ray Horne replace a mile of fence posts. This was greatly appreciated by Ray's three lazy sons who sat around the farmhouse drinking soda pop and listening to the radio all day. For all of his hard work, Zachariah earned plenty of hot meals and continued to help Margie Kittles at the diner.

A few town-folk pitched in a shirt or two and a few odds and ends to help their visiting guest with daily necessities. Sheriff Dan Devine drove down to Independence and asked around hoping to find someone that might know who Zachariah was, but had no luck. The sheriff figured that the quiet stranger was probably a drifter who just happened to wind up in his town. There were plenty of tumbleweeds that blew through the small towns of the Midwest and Sheriff Devine had seen his share. He also knew that Bonnie Parker and Clyde Barrow and their gang were on the run and could be hiding out anywhere. Sheriff Dan looked at the pictures of the members of the Barrow Gang while he was in Montgomery County and Zachariah wasn't one of them. Zachariah was a welcome drifter...so far.

Zachariah was put up in a small garage at Skinny Jim's place
that had been converted to a fairly comfortable, but
temporary, little house. It had a small woodstove, a bed, and
a few spare pictures loaned by Skinny Jim to make if feel
homey. Once again locals like Betty Kinney, Ray Horne's
wife, Mary, and Margie Kittles donated items such as
curtains, books, shaving supplies and the likes. Being as it
was a garage, there were still tools hanging on the walls and
old license plates, but it would do. Zachariah never seemed to
complain about anything anyway.

One day Ray Horne drove Zachariah out to his farm to help
catch a couple calves that had strayed away into the hills
above his place. Zachariah held his arm out of the open side
window of the truck feeling the wind in his hand as they
drove up a long dirt road into the countryside. He noticed a
small house ahead with a man sitting on the porch. As they
neared the house the man stood up and waved at Ray and
Zachariah as they passed. Ray held his hand up like all the
friendly folks from the country do as they go by. Zachariah,
however, kept his eyes on the man even after they passed.
The man was a Native American with long black hair and
was wearing a big wide-brim hat. He had several dogs that
ran out barking at the truck as it went by and continued
chasing it for quite a distance.

Ray Horne, like most folks, spoke to Zachariah even though
they thought he couldn't hear. It was just a little too
uncomfortable spending time with someone and not saying a
word. "That's Henry Coyote," Ray told Zachariah, "he lives
there with his grand-daddy. They've been up here for years

keeping pretty much to themselves. Nice enough fellow though, Osage tribe. A few of 'em scattered around some of these parts. They believe in what they call Wa-kon-tah. When you die your spirit changes into a bird or an animal or some kinda critter, some nonsense like that. They're never any trouble. Those dogs will tear you apart if they have a mind to, sure enough, I guarantee you that.

As the truck made its way up the dirt road leaving a large cloud of dust behind it, Henry Coyote watched until it went over a small hill and out of sight.

LADY'S TEA
Chapter Five

Hazel Spragg's house was a tall Victorian style abode, three stories straight up with two gables on each side. It was a lot of house for just one person and it looked as lonely as she did. Hazel had almost given up any hope of finding a good man in Wheat or anywhere else until the day she laid her eyes on the quiet stranger. The prospect of being with this man in the future was inspiring, and suddenly there was a lot of work that needed to be done at the Spragg mansion.

Zachariah's helpfulness was popular and he was becoming a precious commodity in Wheat. Hazel Spragg wanted to employ Zachariah for her Lady's Tea which she had been planning since the day she saw him. Skinny Jim had hoped to use Zachariah on the same day to move some hay. They argued but Hazel won the heated debate convincing Skinny Jim her need was greater. Skinny Jim's hay would just have to wait.

There would be cucumber sandwiches on pre-sliced Wonder Bread, lemon cookies, meat pie, and Shasta Pale Dry Ginger-ale. While the ladies arrived and found their chairs at lace covered tables in the back yard, Zachariah poured tea and served the guests their snacks from a large silver tray. He looked very dashing and bowed his head handsomely as he presented each guest their portion. Hazel Spragg was in heaven.

Every woman in Wheat, except for Millie Parsons, attended the Lady's Tea. Each one wearing their best dress and behaving as lady-like as a country woman could. Hazel wore long white gloves up to her elbows that were too large which made her look even leaner.

"Nice party," Clara Swanson told Hazel as Zachariah poured her a cup of tea. Clara winked at Hazel who was standing beside Zachariah. It was a wink for good luck. Hazel winked back as if she was smelling victory.

Ray Horne's wife, Mary, along with Ruthie McCabe and Clara Swanson sat together at a small round table with Ray Horne's elderly mother, Francine Horne. Francine had been a true southern belle and at an ornery 90 years old, she still expected to be treated like one. She was not a pleasant person to be with the majority of the time. The Civil War was a sore subject as was any mention of a northern state. In fact, any subject was a bad subject unless it was Francine Horne who brought it up. She had an allergy to everything and she didn't like anything or anybody, at least behind their back. Everyone in Wheat just bit their tongue and let Francine do her complaining routine, everyone but Clara Swanson. Clara enjoyed picking at the old coot.

Betty Kinney brought her three daughters with her and they sat with Margie Kittles. The Kinney girls received a good amount of attention from the ladies in attendance and looked very sweet in their white cotton dresses and large brimmed summer hats. The town had stepped up to the plate in helping the Kinney family since Big Tom had passed. It was what folks did back then during hard times.

Esther Devine sat with Fanny Corbett who brought her daughter-in-law, Liz, who was visiting from Topeka. Ed Morlan's daughter, Flora, showed up late as usual. Flora, like her father, was very intelligent and had attended college, unlike any other female citizen of Wheat. But intellect and common sense in 1933 were two very different qualities and the latter was more acceptable to folks from the country. Rural folks know that courtesy is just plain common sense. Being late wasn't a sin, but always being late was irritating to those who suspected that Flora's poor timing was intentional. Flora's constant tardiness was suspected to be an odd way of getting attention. She never came right out and said it, but there was something about the way Flora Morlan carried herself that made one think that she believed she was better than anyone else.

Hazel Spragg never let Zachariah far out of her watchful eye. She had staked her claim on the man and wasn't about to let any woman have his attention too long. Zachariah seemed to be enjoying his role as servant and charmed each lady with his smile until he reached the table where Francine Horne was seated. Pulling her big brimmed summer hat back, Francine leaned up in her chair to see what Zachariah had on the tray that he was holding in his hand.

"What do you got?" Francine snapped.

"Lemon cookies," Hazel told her as she walked up from behind.

"Oh, Lord, I can't eat those, they give me gas," Francine grumbled. "You got any molasses cookies? I can stomach those."

Hazel tried to be patient with the indignant woman, "No molasses cookies but I can bring you some fresh pie?"

"What kind of pie?" Francine asked suspiciously.

"Well," Hazel answered, "we have meat pie, lemon pie, and apple."

Francine's eyes soured, "Baah, gives me the hives just thinking about them. I'd been better off bringing my own lunch."

Clara Swanson laughed out loud, "There is never a dull moment with you, Francine my dear, never a dull moment."

Francine was offended and hunched back down in her chair with a sour look on her face. As Zachariah walked away to serve other guests Francine asked, "Who is that man, anyway? He looks like a Yankee."

Her daughter-in-law, Mary, answered, "They call him Zachariah, mother, he's a friend of Hazel's. He's helped Ray out on the ranch and I hear he is very helpful."

Francine snorted and insinuated, "I'm sure Hazel is finding him very helpful."

Clara Swanson smiled as she brought the tea cup up to her lips and commented, "I'd bet if he helped you out, Francine, you'd be a much happier woman."

It had been a fine day and every lady, except for Francine Horne, was having a lovely time. For entertainment, Hazel Spragg and Esther Devine prepared to sing "Be Thou My Vision" a hymn they sang together at church the Sunday before. It had been so well received the two decided they would provide an encore performance at the Lady's Tea.

The rest of the ladies gave their full attention as Hazel and Esther began to sing, "Be Thou my vision, O Lord of my heart, naught be all else to me save that Thou art...." Their voices blended beautifully together as they sang in perfect pitch and soothing harmony. Zachariah had been inside the house preparing more tea when the song began, however, before the first verse was finished he appeared back outside and walked slowly towards the singers holding a tea pot in his hand. He stopped and stood in the middle of the crowd with an odd look on his face as though he was thinking deeply about something or listening intently. Suddenly Zachariah looked straight up to the sky and froze like a statue. Hazel and Esther were the first to notice, but then soon others around began to notice as well, except Francine Horne, who was looking around at everyone else trying to figure out what was going on.

Zachariah's eyes were riveted to the sky and soon every lady was looking up and wondering what Zachariah was seeing. Hazel and Esther struggled not to be distracted and continued singing the hymn while occasionally peaking up at the sky too.

Most of the women began to whisper to each other while they watched Zachariah and would sometimes curiously look back up at the sky. Esther quit singing before the last line had been sung, but Hazel managed to finish the final line, "Still be my vision, O ruler of all." By the end of the song the crowd was totally silent until Francine Horne, chewing on a lemon cookie, belched loudly.

Zachariah finally lowered his eyes and realized that everyone was staring at him. He appeared a bit embarrassed, smiled, and then returned into the house.

TROUBLE BEGINS
Chapter Six

It was Tom Corbett's day to "borrow" the very helpful
Zachariah. Tom stopped by Skinny Jim's place early in the
morning to get Zachariah so that he could help him pick up
some bags of fertilizer from the Hardware & Feed. Zachariah
was wearing a brand new pair of bib work overalls that Hazel
Spragg had bought him in return for helping her at the Lady's
Tea.

Tom backed his truck up to the loading dock and then went
inside where Millie and Ernie Parsons were busy with a few
other customers. Zachariah remained outside sitting on the
back of Tom Corbett's truck watching young Willy McCabe
load bags of feed onto a customer's wagon. Willy stacked up
one too many of the burlap sacks onto a wheelbarrow and it
finally surpassed its tipping point .The wheelbarrow toppled
over and the bags came tumbling out. One of the sacks burst
open and grain poured out onto the floor.

Seeing the boy's trouble, Zachariah went over to give him a
hand. "I can do it, Zachariah," Willy told him, "thanks
anyways." Willy was more embarrassed than anything.
Zachariah continued pulling some of the 50 pound bags out
of the way still trying to help the boy. Willy, not realizing
that simply talking louder to a man who can't hear doesn't
matter, repeated himself loudly and more insistently, "You
don't need to do that!" Zachariah looked up at Willy and
smiled as he pulled on one of the burlap sacks totally

unaware of the large man that was coming quickly towards him from behind.

"You leave that boy alone!" shouted Ernie Parsons. Ernie then pushed Zachariah hard causing him to fall onto the floor. Ernie was furious. Zachariah looked frightened and put his arms over his face as he lay on the floor trying to prevent being assaulted again. Ernie stood over Zachariah and pointed at him and with a deep growl warned him, "You stay away from that boy, you freak." Zachariah peeked up at Ernie through his crossed arms and then closed his eyes tight. Willy reared back out of the way to avoid the frightening altercation.

Tom Corbett had witnessed the incident as he was walking outside and shouted, "Hey, what is this?" Tom wasn't happy. "Now come on Ernie, the man was just trying to help the boy."

 Millie Parsons stood by the side door of the business looking confused. She hadn't seen what happened, but she could see her irate husband standing over Zachariah and poor Willy McCabe standing speechless nearby. Young Willy McCabe looked at Ernie wide-eyed and with his mouth standing open in disbelief.

Millie spoke to her husband in a calm voice, "Ernie you need to come inside, it's okay, just come inside."

Ernie Parsons looked back at Millie and then back down at Zachariah who remained on the floor. Ernie was still pointing his finger at Zachariah and his hand was noticeably trembling. Zachariah didn't make a move.

"It's okay Ernie, he was only trying to help," Willy added with a soft and kind voice. Finally, Ernie's body relaxed and he took a deep breath.

"Freak," Ernie grumbled as he walked away and went back inside the hardware store.

Tom Corbett and Willy McCabe helped Zachariah up from the ground. Zachariah looked confused and kept watch on the side door of the business keeping an eye out for Ernie Parsons. It had been an odd scene at Parsons Hardware & Feed. Word got out and most folks that heard about the unfortunate event dismissed it as "Ernie just being Ernie." Some folks thought that there might be more to it and figured Ernie might have known something about Zachariah that people should be concerned about. Be that as it may, the unfortunate matter was forgotten and folks didn't give it a second thought....until it came up again.

BLOOD IN THE STREET
Chapter Seven

It had been about two months since the quiet stranger had
arrived in Wheat. Nearly every citizen had taken advantage
of Zachariah's helpfulness and had come to trust him. Small
towns generally don't welcome strangers. If you're a
newcomer you usually remain a newcomer until your family
has been around for at least two generations. That is just the
way it is. But folks in Wheat took Zachariah under their
wing, for the most part, and he was becoming part of the
community.

It was Thursday afternoon, August 31st, and Zachariah was
helping Clara Swanson peel potatoes for a dinner party she
was having that evening at her house. There was no special
occasion but there was an opportunity to be a good Christian
and share with others. Ray Horne had slaughtered a hog and
gave Clara a nice ham to bake. Clara invited Betty Kinney
and the kids over for dinner. Naturally, Zachariah was
welcome to stay for dinner also, in appreciation for all that he
had done for her. Of course Hazel Spragg managed to invite
herself after learning Zachariah would be there.

Clara helped peel some of the potatoes with Zachariah, and
like everyone else, had a one-way conversation with
Zachariah simply not to feel so awkward. "Oh my, would
you look at that," Clara said as she looked out of her kitchen
window, "those clouds look like they mean business. I
certainly hope so because my garden is dry to the bone."

Clara put down her paring-knife and took off her apron, "I
need to go find my table linens. You're doing real good
Zachariah, I won't be long." Clara then rushed out of the
kitchen while Zachariah started peeling another potato.

Ernie and Millie Parsons were inside the hardware & feed
store alone when the first rain drop hit the roof. It was a large
raindrop that caused both Ernie and Millie to stop what they
were doing and look at each other. It hadn't rained in or near
Wheat for a good spell and there was no rain in the forecast,
at least in the Farmer's Almanac. It wasn't long after the
second big rain drop hit that the third came and then it all
seemed to come down at once. In less than a minute Parsons'
Hardware & Feed was filled with the sound of heavy rain
pounding down on the tin roof. "My word," Millie said in
disbelief, "where did this come from?"

Millie walked towards the back of the store and looked out a
window. The rain was coming down in torrents and the
sound of it on the roof and pounding down on the ground
outside was incredible. Ernie remembered that there were
several sacks of grain outside in front of the store that would
be ruined if they got wet, so he went out to retrieve them.

As he walked out the front door he noticed a man standing in
the street looking at him. The man was drenched by the rain
and was simply standing motionless staring at him. It took a
moment for Ernie to recognize that it was Zachariah.

The rain wasn't letting up. Millie walked behind the counter
to a storage closet and found Ernie's raincoat and put it on.

She knew that she had to help Ernie move some of the goods out of the rain to keep them dry. By the time Millie got to the front door the rain had died down as quickly as it started. She opened the door and stepped outside to find Zachariah kneeling down over her husband who was laying flat on his back with his arms straight out from his sides. Zachariah had his head close to Ernie's and seemed to be whispering something in his ear. Millie was dumbfounded. She then noticed one of Ernie's legs slightly twitching. "Ernie!" Millie shrieked.

 Zachariah was soaking wet and immediately looked up at Millie as if startled. When Zachariah looked up, Millie could clearly see her husband's face and a grotesquely gaping wound in his throat. His eyes were wide open, looking upward but not moving. Ernie's head and upper body were lying in a pool of blood that was quickly mixing with the muddy water that had been left on the street by the sudden rain storm. Millie tried to scream but collapsed unconscious to the porch, overcome by the horrific site.

Zachariah stood up and looked at Ernie and then looked at Millie now crumpled on the porch. Without any expression on his face, Zachariah looked back down at the dead man while the low dark clouds in the sky, that seemed to have appeared from nowhere, moved onward to the west. Like the clouds leaving, Zachariah just walked away.

The news of the murder of Ernie Parsons hit the locals as fast and hard as a bolt of lightning. The shock brought a wave of fear, disbelief, and for the first time for most, a sense of vulnerability in the community. Until then no one locked their doors in Wheat. Other than an occasional stray dog roaming town or a loose bull there had never been any problems, least anyone could recall. Now, one of their own had been brutally murdered and it was as if the blood was on their hands. The good people of Wheat had willingly allowed a stranger into their homes and he killed their friend. They felt betrayed and at the same time guilty for being so naive.

The Dixon County Building was the oldest building in Wheat. It had been a slaughterhouse in the last century and donated to the good people of Wheat in 1901. It had two jail cells, one used mainly for storage. There was a small office that the Sheriff used on occasion to do his paperwork, as was required by county ordinances. The Dixon County Building also had a good sized room for council meetings, which doubled for Bingo on every other Thursday night, and a large hall used as a courtroom. Other than Bingo, the Dixon County Building was rarely used for anything.

Ed Morlan, who was one of the three county commissioners, met with Sheriff Dan in the council room at seven o'clock that evening. Tom Corbett and Herb Tobin, the other two commissioners arrived shortly after. There were lots of questions that needed to be answered and the men had to mentally change their focus from being simply local citizens to being community leaders. It was a call to duty, and for each man it was like an old horse getting up off the ground and shaking the dirt out of its coat before it could get moving again.

"Where is he?" Tom Corbett asked the sheriff.

"He's in back locked up," the sheriff answered. "It took me awhile to find the key, but he wasn't going anywhere. He acts like nothing has happened."

"Where did you find him?" Herb Tobin added.

"He was sitting in his little place behind Skinny Jim's. He followed me over here and sat down and waited until I could find the key to the jail cell to let him in and that's where he is now."

Herb Tobin had once been a lawyer before coming to Wheat twenty years earlier. He knew a little about crime investigation and evidence for court purposes. "Did you find a knife or whatever was used to cut his throat, Dan?"

The sheriff took off his hat and ran his fingers through his hair. "No, I didn't, and the funny part is, I didn't find a lick of blood on him anywhere. In fact, his clothes weren't even wet. Millie told me that he was soaked to the bone standing in the middle of the rain storm when this happened outside the hardware and feed store. It couldn't have been more than twenty minutes after he killed Ernie that I arrested him. Millie said he was wearing the same white cotton suit with the red and blue tie that he's wearing now, but something don't figure."

"Where's Ernie?" Tom Corbett asked.

Sheriff Dan put his hat back on. "I got him bundled up in a tarp out back in my truck. Ray Horne was driving by, thank God, and helped me load him up. Margie Kittles took Millie home, she's a mess as you could imagine, poor gal. Tom, I'm going to have you stay here with Zachariah while I take Ernie's body down to Independence. Don't let nobody in while I'm gone. If someone has something to say about this, let them know that I'll be talking to them as soon as I get back."

Herb Tobin was thinking ahead, "We need to get our heads together on how to try this Mr. Zachariah and how to handle all of the legal matters that will come up. We don't even have a judge anymore."

The sheriff nodded his head in agreement, "I agree with you there, Herb, but I still have an investigation to do and for now I'm detaining him on suspicion of the murder of Ernie Parsons. While you're all here, why don't you have an official meeting and find us a judge and figure some of those things out, I got some business to take care of. Remember, Tom, nobody gets in. There's a shotgun beside my desk. Make yourselves a pot of coffee and I'll see ya'll in bit."

THE HONORABLE GROVER T. CRABTREE
Chapter Eight

Traveling judges weren't unheard of in 1933 in Kansas, but finding an available one wasn't easy. Herb Tobin finally located a retired judge in Wichita by the name of, Grover T. Crabtree, who agreed to rule at the trial of 'State of Kansas vs. John Doe Zachariah'. The judge agreed because the case had all the elements for making the news. It was everything that news and magazine readers enjoyed, a dicey blood curdling murder by a mysterious stranger in a small town.

The Honorable Grover T. Crabtree was a salty little man with piercing blue eyes and a full head of thick white hair. His booming voice was three times as big as he was. Judge Crabtree enjoyed his authority and the notoriety his position gave him. He especially loved to see his name in the newspapers and never let the opportunity for posing for a camera pass him by. Crabtree's ability to market his name had earned him his judicial position in the beginning. He could turn a traffic ticket into headline news with one phone call. Since this would be Crabtree's last trial he made sure that he would go out in a glorious explosion of flashbulbs from the cameras of every press reporter within five hundred miles.

The commissioners of Dixon County insisted that the trial be held in their own county. The costs to hire a judge, prosecutor, defense lawyer, bailiff, and to house jurors would be enormous, but the local farmers did well for themselves and the county funds were available. To hand off Ernie Parsons' death to some other county wouldn't do. It was Wheat's responsibility for Ernie's justice and justice would be served.

Judge Crabtree called for a closed hearing on Monday, September 4th, in the Dixon County Building's courtroom. The courtroom was cleaned up and more chairs were brought in to accommodate an anticipated large gallery.

Zachariah was brought in before Judge Crabtree so that the judge could decide if Zachariah was capable and competent to be tried for Murder in the 1st Degree. Sheriff Dan Devine brought Zachariah into the courtroom and sat him down on a chair in front of the judge's bench. Zachariah's feet were shackled together and his hands were in handcuffs in front of him. He appeared to be concentrating on trying to walk with the awkward shackles around his ankles, but once he sat down in the chair he looked up at the judge and showed his well known innocent smile. For a moment the judge fell for the smile and smiled back at Zachariah but then quickly returned to his serious piercing eyes look.

Richard W. Davis from Wichita had been loaned to Dixon County to act as Prosecutor for the State of Kansas. Mr. Davis was an experienced trial lawyer who was known to be a crack-shot in the courtroom. He was young for a lawyer and highly educated in law, confident, skilled, and accomplished. John Fry had been appointed to defend Zachariah. Fry had his own practice in Independence and although he didn't have much trial experience, he had a sincere passion in defending the rights of indigent people who could use his help. John Fry, like the prosecutor Richard Davis, had not met the accused Mr. Zachariah and both were anxious to examine the quiet stranger.

"All right gentleman," Judge Crabtree announced, "you've all had a chance to meet each other, so now I would like to know more about this man, Mr. Zachariah. I am told that he cannot hear or speak and apparently he cannot read either. So I am curious to know how he functions at all. The judge turned toward the sheriff, "Sheriff Devine does this man dress himself?"

The sheriff straightened up his back and answered, "Yes sir, your Honor, he does."

The judge looked Zachariah over, "Well, his shoes are tied and he can put on a necktie, so obviously he has something going on. How does he fend for himself? Does he have a job?"

Sheriff Devine answered, "He gets by. He's been working for folks doing odd jobs and different sorts of chores. The folks around here have been…had been…helping him out, paying him here and there for some of his work and making him lunch and dinners and such."

"So let me get this straight," the judge continued, "this Zachariah fellow came into town a couple of months ago, nobody knows who he is and you took the man into your homes?"

The sheriff's eyes looked towards the floor with embarrassment and he replied humbly, "He didn't seem to be much of a threat to anyone, your Honor, and is...or was actually...quite helpful."

Judge Crabtree raised his bushy eyebrows and shook his head in disgust and then turned to Zachariah. "Mr. Zachariah, do you hear anything that I am saying?" the judge asked loudly.

Zachariah didn't say anything but gave a slight smile. "Do you understand anything I am saying?" the judge asked clearly and insistently.

Zachariah remained silent and pleasant. "Very well," the judge went on, "I find that this man is capable of standing trial in this matter. We'll begin in two weeks, which should give you both enough time to prepare your cases and select your jurors."

"How am I supposed to defend this man, your honor?" Mr. Fry asked, "How am I supposed to communicate with him?"

The judge sat up in his chair and with a calm but flat voice answered, "It seems the people of Wheat didn't have much of a problem communicating with Mr. Zachariah, Mr. Fry. I suggest you ask them any questions you might have. Sheriff Devine will give you a list of his witnesses and you can start there. Now if there aren't any more questions this hearing is adjourned."

Mr. Fry shook his head. He knew he wouldn't get much sympathy from the judge. Crabtree had a bulldog reputation and was just another prosecutor wearing a black robe.

THE TRIAL BEGINS
Chapter Nine

The courtroom at the Dixon County Building on the first day of trial was about half full. It hadn't rained a drop since the day Ernie Parsons was murdered and it was still hot for mid-September. However the thick stone and brick walls of the Dixon County Building kept its occupants relatively cool as long as the front doors weren't left open and nobody breathed.

Zachariah sat at the defense table beside his attorney, John Fry, with his hands folded on top of the table and a perplexed look on his face. Mr. Fry nervously went through some of the paperwork on the table in front of him trying to sort his thoughts.

The jury consisted of nine men and three women from Montgomery County. A thirteenth juror sat in a chair on the end of the juror's seats as an alternate in the event there was a problem with one of the other jurors.

Sheriff Devine was acting as bailiff. His job began as soon as Judge Crabtree arrived through a side door where his make-shift chambers had been created. "All rise, the Honorable Grover T. Crabtree residing, the State of Kansas vs. Mr. John Doe Zachariah is now in session."

Judge Crabtree made his way to his chair as if he was a proud Olympian, cape flowing behind, making his way to the victory platform. As soon as the judge sat down he had everyone else sit back down and then went straight to business, "Mr. Davis, your first witness."

Mr. Davis stood up at his table and called, "The state would like to call Miss Margaret Kittles."

Herb Tobin opened the front door of the courtroom where Margie was waiting in a front lobby and let her know it was her time to testify. Herb had been allowed in the courtroom because he was not being called as a witness in this case. He had never met Zachariah until the day Zachariah was arrested and put in jail. Herb had been out of town visiting family in Ohio the entire time the quiet stranger had been in Wheat.

Margie walked into the courtroom and nervously pulled back the strand of hair that habitually fell into her face. She actually looked very attractive and was wearing make-up and a flower patterned dress that was tangerine orange in color with matching high-heeled shoes. She walked up to the bench and was met by Sheriff Devine who swore her in, "Do you promise to tell the truth, the whole truth and nothing but the truth, so help you God?"

Margie looked at the sheriff with one eyebrow raised, "Of course I do, Dan," and then walked over to the witness chair and sat down to look at all the faces looking back at her.

The prosecutor stood up from behind his table and tapped on his hand with a pencil as he spoke, "Good morning, Miss Kittles."

Margie didn't like the way the man was smiling at her. She could tell when she was being patronized and Richard W. Davis looked like a young city slicker who was too big for his britches. "Mornin'," Margie answered dryly.

The prosecutor detected a slight chill from the witness so he moved around his desk to come closer to her to try to win her over. "I understand that you own and operate the local diner here in Wheat, is that right?" he asked.

"I do." Margie answered.

"And do you know that man sitting beside counsel over there?" he asked.

Margie turned to Zachariah and looked at him quickly and then lowered her eyes. "I do." Margie replied almost as if ashamed of her answer.

"And what is his name?" the prosecutor asked.

"Zachariah," Margie answered softly, "least that's what people call him around here." Margie had a hard time looking into Zachariah's eyes. She had mixed feelings that were hard to deal with. She had come to really like the quiet stranger and now found it hard to believe she was looking into the eyes of a cold blooded murderer.

Mr. Davis came closer to Margie and leaned his elbow up on the rail beside her. "That's what people call him around here. Do you know his real name?"

Margie shook her head and replied, "No, I don't."

"All right then, where did he get this name "Zachariah" that everyone refers to him by?" the prosecutor asked.

Margie shrugged her shoulders, "I don't know for sure, I guess someone just gave him the name because we didn't know his real one."

 "Mr. Davis walked slowly back toward his chair and asked, "So tell me Miss Kittles, what is this man's real name?"

John Fry stood up and interrupted the prosecutor, "Objection, your Honor, this witness already said that she didn't know his name."

Judge Crabtree lowered his chin and looked over his glasses at the prosecutor, "She did already answer that question, Mr. Davis, go on to the next question."

Mr. Davis gave a cocky grin and walked back toward Margie who wiggled slightly to sit up straight in her chair and be ready for the next question. "Tell me, Miss Kittles, how you came to know the defendant, Mr. Zachariah."

Margie took a deep breath and then answered him, "Well, he came into my diner one morning about two months ago. I remember the day well because we learned that Big Tom Kin...Tom Kinney had died next door in the garage of his filling station. Zachariah just walked in out of nowhere and he's been around ever since."

Two of the female jurors quickly looked at each other when Margie mentioned Big Tom Kinney's death. The prosecutor noticed the two jurors' reaction and felt he was onto something.

"Tom Kinney, a friend of yours Miss Kittles?" the prosecutor asked. "How did he die?"

Mr. Fry objected, "Objection your Honor, this has no relevance to this matter and Miss Kittles isn't qualified to answer that question in the first place."

"Sustained," replied the judge, "move on, Mr. Davis."

The prosecutor knew the question would get an objection but it didn't matter, the jury surely could put two and two together. "Miss Kittles, it is my understanding that the defendant worked for you at times, is that right?"

Margie nodded, "That's right, at times."

"And correct me if I am wrong, he helped you prepare food for your customers at the diner?" the prosecutor asked.

Margie took her time before she answered the question and wondered where the prosecutor was going with the question. "At times." She finally answered.

Mr. Davis once again came over beside Margie and put his elbow up on the rail beside her, "Was he a good worker, good at what you had him do?"

Margie nodded, "Yes, he was a very good worker."

"Tell me, Miss Kittles, what kind of food do you serve at your diner." Margie thought to herself a minute and ran down the menu in her mind, "Sandwiches, soup, breakfasts, eggs, bacon and so on, sometimes we'll have ham or roast beef…coffee…ginger ale…'bout anything I guess."

The prosecutor smiled and commented trying to schmooze the jurors, "Mmm, that sounds good right now, you're making us all hungry. And so the defendant, Mr. Zachariah, helped you prepare this food?"

Margie shrugged one of her shoulders and answered, "Yep, he did."

"All right," answered the prosecutor, "tell me this if you would, what kind of kitchen utensils does it take to prepare a ham or a roast beef sandwich?"

Margie now knew where Mr. Davis was going with his questioning. So did Mr. Fry, "Objection," Mr. Fry called out in frustration.

Mr. Davis disagreed, "It's a relevant question your Honor, we know the victim's throat was cut and it stands to reason that the defendant had access to objects sharp enough to cause that sort of wound."

"I'll allow Miss Kittles to answer that question, but let's move on Mr. Davis." The judge urged.

Mr. Davis moved over towards the jurors and faced them. "Miss Kittles, did Mr. Zachariah use knives to prepare food for your customers?"

Again Margie cautiously answered, "Yes, he did."

"Were they sharp knives?" Mr. Davis asked.

"Yes, they are all sharp knives," Margie answered as if weary.

"All right," the prosecutor said, "so would it be safe to say that Mr. Zachariah was pretty good with a sharp knife?"

"Objection," howled Mr. Fry.

The judge was also a little frustrated with Mr. Davis' line of questioning. He'd seen many a fancy-pants prosecutors and attorneys in his time and wasn't impressed by them. "Sustained, Mr. Davis, let's not go down this road again." The judge told him.

Mr. Davis gave a sheepish grin and apologized before returning to his chair. "Yes, your Honor, I have no further questions for this witness at this time."

The judge looked over at Margie and then to Mr. Fry. "Mr. Fry, your cross."

"Thank you, your Honor," Mr. Fry said politely as he approached the witness stand. "Good morning, Miss Kittles."

"Good morning." Margie said.

"How often did Mr. Zachariah help you at the diner?" the attorney asked.

Margie looked upward recalling the past two months, "Maybe two, three times a week, sometimes more, sometimes less, I suppose."

Mr. Fry continued, "During that time have you ever seen Mr. Zachariah behave as a danger to anyone, a threat to anyone?"

Margie didn't have to give it any thought and answered, "No."

Mr. Fry went on, "In fact, have you ever seen or heard of Mr. Zachariah being violent towards anyone outside of what happened to Ernest Parsons?"

Margie took in a breath and answered, "No, I have not."

John Fry did not have a good case. Good cases were like a good hand at cards. You either got a good hand and bet big or you got a bad hand and had to bluff. This hand was the latter. However, sometimes one card can change the turn of the entire game. John Fry received a surprise in the next card he was dealt.

"Where were you on the afternoon, early evening of Thursday, August 31st of this year, Miss. Kittles?"

Margie answered without hesitation. "We were at the diner finishing up, I was going to go play Bingo and Zachariah was cleaning up for me."

The judge and prosecutor who had been listening and looking at paperwork in front of them looked over at Miss Kittles on the stand with heightened interest. Margie just sat and waited for the next question.

Mr. Fry repeated himself, "I'm sorry, Miss Kittles, maybe you misheard me. I asked what you were doing on the afternoon, early evening of Thursday August 31st last month? Do you remember anything of significance on that date?"

Margie pulled in her chin, "Of course I do, that was the night they found Ernie Parsons dead, like I said, I was at the diner with Zachariah getting ready to go play Bingo and…"

Mr. Fry interrupted, "Are you certain of the date, Miss Kittles, are you sure of that?"

Margie Kittles then interrupted Mr. Fry. "Sure I'm sure. It rained so hard that we couldn't go outside. The sky just opened up and turned the streets into mud. Rained so hard we couldn't have Bingo that night because the roof here leaked so badly."

John Fry was baffled and speechless. This wasn't at all what he had expected to hear. Miss Kittles seemed to be an honest person, but maybe there was something going on and she was covering up for Zachariah. "At what time did you finally leave the diner that evening Miss Kittles?" Mr. Fry asked.

Margie pulled back the strand of hair that had fallen in her face again and answered, "Ohhh, about an hour after the rain stopped. I went on home and Zachariah went on towards Skinny Jim's where he lives."

Mr. Fry raised his eyebrows and stood in front of the witness staring at her for an awkwardly long moment in confusion. "I have no further questions, your Honor."

The judge turned toward Mr. Davis who was anxious to ask further questions. "Miss Kittles, what was the defendant, Mr. Zachariah, wearing when he left the diner?"

Margie thought for a moment and then said, "He was wearing a clean white shirt and his overalls that Hazel Spragg bought him. Oh, and while he was working he was wearing a white apron, he always wears an apron when he works at the diner. He hung up his apron just before we left."

Mr. Davis sensed that Margie Kittles was not being truthful. Millie Parsons was certain that Zachariah had been wearing his white suit coat and white cotton suit pants. And there was no question that it was raining when Ernie Parsons walked out of the Hardware & Feed Store when he was murdered. Mr. Davis was no longer smiling and being charming. He wasn't about to start this trial with a witness lying on the stand. "Miss Kittles, I want to make sure that before you leave here today you understand the importance of the truthfulness of your testimony. A man has been murdered in cold blood. Now, you have sworn an oath to give the truth. Are you familiar with perjury?"

Margie Kittles wasn't a college educated woman, but she wasn't an idiot, and she certainly wasn't going to be accused of perjury by some spoiled city boy. She pointed her finger at the prosecutor and made herself very clear, "Mr. Davis, if you want to call me a liar then you had better come out and just say it. Ernie and Millie Parsons have been good friends of mine for many years and I wouldn't lie for anyone, especially for any murderer. I am not a liar so don't you even get me started."

Judge Crabtree tried to hide his smile by covering his mouth with one of his hands. Looking over his glasses he asked Mr. Davis, who was trying to compose himself, "Any further questions for this witness, Mr. Davis?"

The prosecutor started to say something but then answered in frustration, "No. I have no further questions with this witness."

"Since there are no further questions at this time, the court will take a fifteen minute break," Judge Crabtree responded.

The big room filled with a rumble of whispers from the gallery. Everyone could sense the beginning of a very strange trial.

DAMAGING TESTIMONY
Chapter Ten

The trial of Zachariah reconvened after the break. Ed Morlan was sworn in and took a long drink of water from a glass that was sitting on a table beside the witness stand. Ed looked around the room as he swiveled in his chair and focused through his thick glasses checking out the jurors.

Mr. Davis began his direct questioning as he walked up towards Ed Morlan reading from a notepad, "Mr. Morlan, how long have you lived here in Wheat?"

Ed put down his glass of water, "Probably before your parents were born, son, I've been here a long, long time."

The prosecutor smiled. He enjoyed witnesses that were old-timers. They were honest and had nothing to lose. "Then there would be no doubt that you know just about everyone here in Dixon County, would I be right about that, Mr. Morlan?"

Ed nodded his head, "Every man, woman, and child."

The prosecutor continued, "And so you obviously knew Big Tom Kinney, is that right, Mr. Morlan."

Ed Morlan shook his head solemnly and answered with a soft low voice, "Yes, I knew Big Tom, I knew him well. He was a good friend and a good man."

Mr. Davis, pretending to be empathetic replied, "I am sure he was, Mr. Morlan, I am sure he was. By the way, Mr. Morlan, have you ever seen this man before, sitting next to Mr. Fry?"

Mr. Davis looked over at Zachariah leading Ed Morlan's attention to the defendant.

"Yes, I have," Ed Morlan replied.

Mr. Davis then walked up quickly to Ed Morlan pointing his finger at Zachariah, "Would you tell the court when you saw Mr. Zachariah for the very first time, the very first time you ever laid eyes on him?"

Ed Morlan looked over at Zachariah for a moment and focused his eyes on him. He then answered the question, "The first time I saw this man was when he walked out of Big Tom Kinney's filling station. It was after hours. Dan Devine…Sheriff Dan Devine found Big Tom dead a few hours later inside the garage of his filling station."

The courtroom filled with sounds of loud murmuring that were abruptly quieted when Judge Crabtree brought down his gavel and demanded silence.

"Objection," John Fry called out, "hearsay, Mr. Morlan has no firsthand knowledge of when and what the sheriff found."

A news reporter from Wichita was in the gallery waiting for some action. He stood up and took a photograph of Ed

Morlan on the stand while Mr. Davis and Mr. Fry argued about Morlan's testimony. The reporter had received a tip from a certain retired judge that the Zachariah trial might be newsworthy. So far the scoop was good.

By noon on the first day of the trial, the inside of the courtroom was already becoming too warm. Some of the spectators fanned themselves with anything they could find to do the job. Sheriff Dan, the bailiff, no longer was wearing his jacket and rolled up his sleeves to stay cooler. He figured he'd been around long enough that he didn't have to impress anyone. Mr. Davis remained looking cool and calm in his black three piece suit while John Fry eventually removed his suit jacket and loosened his tie. Mr. Fry was perspiring badly too. It was becoming a very difficult first day for the defense and would only get worst.

Pete Barnes was the first to testify after the lunch break. After Sheriff Devine had sworn him in, Pete sat down in the witness chair and looked ready to go. He was wearing his Sunday best overalls with a white shirt and a country bow tie. Although Pete was probably the most prosperous man in the region, wearing a suit never appealed to him. He considered himself a working man and wasn't going to pretend he was anyone else.

"Good afternoon, Mr. Barnes," the prosecutor began.

Pete Barnes nodded his head to acknowledge the man.

The prosecutor then asked, "Can you tell the court how long you have lived here in Wheat?"

Pete Barnes tapped his fingers on the arms of the chair and thought about the question briefly and then said, "I have been in this county all my life as was my father."

Mr. Davis returned in front of the jury and went on with his questions, "So it would be safe to say that you know everyone around this area, would that be true?"

"It would," Pete answered.

"And you also know the defendant, Mr. Zachariah?" the prosecutor asked.

"I do," Pete replied without hesitation and without shame.

"When was the first time you met this Mr. Zachariah?" asked the prosecutor.

Pete Barnes looked directly at Zachariah, "I saw him for the first time over at Margie Kittles' diner, must have been around six in the morning. I know it was the first Friday of the month and that would have been the 7th, the 7th of July. Margie has a Breakfast Special on Fridays and I bought Zachariah breakfast."

The prosecutor tilted his head, put his hand on his hip and leaned backwards as if he couldn't believe what he was hearing, "Are you saying that you bought a complete stranger a meal? Why would you do that?"

Pete Barnes looked at the prosecutor and then back at Zachariah who smiled at him, "Oh, it was just the Good Samaritan thing to do, I suppose. He couldn't talk, couldn't read, we figured someone dumped him in town and I figured he could use some grub. Weren't no harm in that."

Mr. Davis nodded his head in agreement, "No harm at the time anyway, right Mr. Barnes?"

Mr. Fry stopped Pete before he could answer, "Objection."

"Sustained," agreed the judge.

"So you just testified that you figured someone had dumped the defendant in town, do you remember saying that Mr. Barnes?"

Pete nodded, "I do."

"So obviously if someone is dumped they wouldn't have an automobile, would you agree with that?"

Pete nodded again and answered, "He didn't have an automobile, none that I could see around anyways. He just showed up at Margie's and that's all I know."

The prosecutor walked up closer to Pete Barnes and asked him, "Do you own an automobile, Mr. Barnes?"

"I own a 1925 Ford, Model T, it's a flatbed." Pete answered.

Mr. Davis retreated back in front of the jurors and smiled at them to get their attention, "You ever had Big Tom Kinney work on your truck Mr. Barnes?"

"Yes, a couple of times, Pete answered, " I had him replace some bearings in one of the wheels on that truck and he replaced my tires about a year ago."

Mr. Davis slowly ran his hand down the rail in front of the jurors, "If someone was a complete stranger in this town and had no automobile, can you think of any reason they would walk out of Big Tom Kinney's filling station after business hours?"

John Fry shot up out of his seat and loudly objected, "Objection your Honor, argumentative."

The judge agreed, "Sustained, Mr. Davis, enough of that."

Mr. Davis smirked, "Fair enough," and walked back behind his desk. "Mr. Barnes, who else did you have breakfast with at Margie Kittles on the morning of Friday, July 7th?"

Pete thought for a moment and with his eyes raised upward he began recalling the others, "Well, Margie was there of course, Zachariah was there sitting by himself by the window, Dan Devine was there for a short spell, and Ed

Morlan came in after Dan left. I think that was all that was there that I can remember, least while I was there."

"Was there someone missing, Mr. Barnes? Someone who never missed a Friday morning Breakfast Special at Margie's Diner, was there *anyone* that was not there on Friday, July 7th?"

Pete lowered his eyes and after a quiet pause gave his sad response, "Big Tom wasn't there."

"And where was he, Mr. Barnes?" the prosecutor demanded.

"Objection!" John Fry shouted.

The judge looked over his glasses at Mr. Davis with a raised eyebrow. Mr. Davis knew he was pushing his luck, "No further questions your Honor."

John Fry rubbed one of his eyes before he stood up. He picked up his notepad and pencil and walked up to the witness stand and nodded a greeting to Pete Barnes. Pete nodded back. "How well do you know Mr. Zachariah, Mr. Barnes?"

Pete looked back over at Zachariah, "As well as you can know somebody in a few weeks, I reckon'. I mean I don't know where he comes from, but he worked for me quite a bit helping around the farm and the house."

Mr. Fry wrote down the answer on his notepad. "What kind of worker was Zachariah, was he a good worker?"

"Yes, he was a good worker, a hard worker to tell you the truth, he was…very helpful."

Mr. Fry had noticed that description before and repeated it, "Very helpful. Did Zachariah ever give you any trouble?"

Pete Barnes raised his eyes for a short moment to think and then replied, "No, never gave me any trouble."

"Did he ever give you any cause to be concerned for your safety?" Fry asked.

Pete Barnes shook his head, "No, not me."

"Were you there at Parsons Hardware & Feed when Ernest Parsons was killed?" Mr. Fry asked out of the blue.

Pete Barnes squinted his eyes and wondered why the attorney would ask such a dumb question, "No, of course not."

"When was the last time you left Dixon County and went anywhere, Mr. Barnes?"

Pete Barnes answered proudly, "I haven't left this county for over 20 years. No need to."

John Fry walked up in front of the counsel's desk and sat on the corner of it, "You're a farmer by trade, so I am assuming that you pay close attention to the weather around here, would I be accurate in saying that?"

Pete Barnes agreed, "I am and I do."

"So, can you tell me how many times it has rained…say in the last three months here in this area?" Fry asked.

"Once," Barnes answered quickly.

" Can you tell me more about that?" Fry prodded.

"We were out by Verdigris River Road looking for arrowheads when all of a sudden it just started raining. It come out of nowhere, clouds rolled in, we got drenched and it turned the road into a soggy mess. We jumped back in the truck and waited it out, oh, it must have lasted only five minutes or so, then we started heading back. Got stuck though for a bit."

Once again Judge Crabtree and Mr. Davis's attention perked up. This did not make any sense at all.

Mr. Fry continued on with his questioning, "Mr. Barnes, you just referred to "we" when you were giving your testimony. Were you with someone else out on Verdigris River Road?"

Pete didn't give it a second thought and answered directly, "It was me and Zachariah. Zachariah went with me. He helped me install some cabinets in my kitchen so I figured I'd treat him to some exploring up by the river and maybe find some arrowheads. There's lots of 'em up there, you know."

John Fry was feeling pretty good about Pete Barnes' testimony. "No further questions with this witness."

Mr. Davis got up quickly from his chair with a puzzled look on his face. "Mr. Barnes, how far away is Verdigris River Road from the town of Wheat?"

Pete squinted one eye and gave it some thought, "Oh, I'd say it's about eight, nine miles out and northwest of here. Half that is pretty slow going though, roads up there aren't too good."

The prosecutor approached Pete slowly and asked another question, "What time was it when it rained."

Pete shrugged his shoulders, "Couldn't tell you, I don't carry a watch, it was sometime late afternoon, I spec'."

"You don't carry a watch," the prosecutor mumbled to himself. "Then let me ask you this, Mr. Barnes, what was Mr. Zachariah wearing at the time you were out on this little exploration." Mr. Davis was getting impatient.

Pete answered him, "He was wearing a pair of bib overalls. I think he only has two sets of clothes, them bibs and that white suit he's wearing."

Mr. Davis was now very hot. The room was a furnace and the breathing air was running low. "Mr. Barnes, do you remember you and I speaking about your testimony just the other day right here in this building?"

"Sure I do," Pete replied.

"Why did you not tell me about this drive up to Verdigris River Road when you talked to me just two days ago?"

Pete could see that Mr. Davis' fur was raised up on his back, but wasn't about to take the blame, "You never asked me," Pete said calmly.

The prosecutor turned toward the judge as if looking for someone to bail him out. The judge only raised his eyebrows and shook his head as if he was ashamed of Mr. Davis for not doing his job. "No further questions," Mr. Davis said in disgust as he walked back to his chair.

Judge Crabtree then announced, "Okay, we are done for the day. It's getting too hot in here to think. We'll start tomorrow morning earlier, say 8:00 a.m. sharp and hopefully the hot air in this room will be cleared out by then." Mr. Davis looked up at the judge wondering if he was referring to him. Turning towards the jury the judge reminded them, "Remember, do not discuss this case with anyone and do not do any investigating on your own. We'll see you all back here in the morning."

"All rise," Dan Devine announced as the judge went to his chambers.

While the jurors were moving towards the exit doors Mr. Davis walked over to the defense table where Zachariah and Mr. Fry were standing. Sheriff Dan stood and waited a short distance away to take Zachariah back to his jail cell. "What are you trying to pull, John," Davis demanded keeping his voice low.

Mr. Fry straightened out the paperwork on the desk in front of him and chuckled, "It's all new to me."

The prosecutor put his hands down on the front of the desk and bent over slightly between Mr. Fry and Zachariah and warned them, "I am going to get down to the bottom of this. There is no way one man can be in three different places at once."

"They are your witnesses, Mr. Davis;" Fry told him plainly. "Sheriff, Mr. Zachariah is ready to go with you." John Fry picked up his paperwork and put it in his attaché case and walked out of the building. Sheriff Dan nodded to Zachariah to have him follow him and Zachariah walked slowly and carefully around the prosecutor who was obviously very irritated and staring Zachariah in the eyes.

COURTROOM DRAMA
Chapter Eleven

A few miles west of Kansas City, Virginia Rayburne sat in her wheelchair waiting for her morning tea. It had been five years since the horrible automobile accident that had taken her husband's life. The fiery collision had left grotesque burn scars over most of Virginia's body including her face. In addition to the terrible burns, the woman's back had been broken and she no longer had use of her legs. Once a promising dancer, her natural youthful beauty had been stolen away. Virginia Rayburne went from a beautiful and popular socialite to a lonely and sad recluse to avoid the constant and hurtful stares. Fortunately her husband had made a small fortune while he was alive and Mrs. Rayburne was well off financially.

While waiting for her tea, her assistant Tess, placed the morning newspaper on the table in front of her. Mrs. Rayburne rolled her wheelchair closer to the table and picked up the folded newspaper and laid it on her lap. She looked out at the sunshine coming through her window and sighed. It was a beautiful morning but it would be just another boring day inside a lonely house for Virginia Rayburne. Tess brought in the cup of hot tea on a saucer and placed it on the table and then quickly returned to the kitchen to start breakfast. Mrs. Rayburne unfolded the newspaper with her badly scarred left hand while picking up her teacup with her right hand. A photograph of President Roosevelt waving from a yacht made the front page which was nothing new.

Political news was of no interest, however, a man wearing a white suit in a picture on the bottom right side of the front page took Mrs. Rayburne's breath away. She stared at the man's picture as if in shock. It was a photograph taken in a court room and the caption above read, "Mystery Man Murder Trial." Mrs. Rayburne had seen this man before and she nearly fainted as her teacup went crashing to the floor.

Tom Corbett was the first to take the stand on the second day of the trial at 8:00 a.m. sharp. He was sworn in by the sheriff and avoided looking towards Zachariah. Tom was a confident and successful man on most days, but today he seemed very nervous and it was obvious that he didn't want to be on the witness stand.

"Good morning, Mr. Corbett," the prosecutor said loudly as he went to work on the witness.

Tom Corbett cleared his throat a couple of times and managed a shaky reply, "Good morning."

"Mr. Corbett," the prosecutor began, "do you know the man in the white suit sitting next to Mr. Fry at counsel's table?"

"Yes, I do, sort of." Tom answered.

"Tell me about that, Mr. Corbett, how do you know him?"

Tom Corbett kept his eyes fixed on Mr. Davis, "I met him not long after he came into town. I heard he was a pretty good worker so I had him help me with fixen' some fences, painting, some simple work here and there."

"I see," said Mr. Davis. "During that time have you ever heard him say a word to anyone?"

Tom Corbett shook his head and said, "No, I haven't."

"Can he hear?" asked the prosecutor.

Tom shrugged his shoulders, "I don't know, sometimes he seems to. I don't know if he can read lips, I just don't know. I show him what I want done and he just does it."

Mr. Davis approached the witness stand and held his arms out to his side, "So the man is not ignorant, he's capable of doing anything you ask him to. Is that right Mr. Corbett?"

John Fry objected and argued that Tom Corbett was not qualified to answer the question, however, the judge did not agree. "Answer the question, Mr. Corbett."

"As far as I can tell he's an intelligent person," Tom answered.

"Mr. Corbett did you know the decedent, Ernest Parsons?" the prosecutor asked.

"Yes, I knew Ernie," Tom answered.

"Ernie Parsons a good man?" Mr. Davis asked.

Tom nodded his head while he thought about the question and replied, "Yes, I'd say he was a good man."

Mr. Davis walked up close to the witness stand and looked at Tom for a moment and finally asked, "Did Ernie have some *difficulties* at times, Mr. Corbett?"

Tom scooted up in his seat and looked uncomfortable and didn't answer. "Let me put it this way," Mr. Davis pressed on, "have you ever seen Ernest Parsons rough anyone up, ever?"

Tom cleared his throat a couple of times but no words were coming out, "Umm, well, umm."

Mr. Davis reminded the witness, "Remember, you are under oath here, Mr. Corbett, you are here to tell the truth and nothing but the truth."

Tom looked over at Ernie Parsons' in-laws who were in the gallery. Finally he cleared his throat one more time and answered the question, "I have."

Mr. Davis smiled knowing that he had opened the door he was knocking on. "Tell me about that Mr. Corbett, tell the court what you witnessed."

Tom took a deep breath and spoke, "Ernie went to the war and came back different. He, he wasn't the same when he come home. He was quieter, not so happy-go-lucky like he used to be, I guess, and sometimes he was just a hot head. He wasn't like the old Ernie. Anyways, about the first of last month I took Zachariah over to his place, the Hardware & Feed Store, to pick up some things. Something happened outside between Ernie and Zachariah and a boy from here in town. Ernie got real mad and knocked Zachariah down on the ground. I guess Ernie thought that Zachariah was bothering the boy, but I don't think he was. But that's just Ernie. So after all that, I took Zachariah back home. That was about it."

Mr. Davis nodded his head and repeated what the witness had said, "That was about it...Thank you, Mr. Corbett. Now, were you with Zachariah on that day it rained so hard here in Wheat?"

Tom Corbett replied confidently, "No, I was not with Zachariah at the time the rain came down."

Mr. Davis smiled, "Thank you, Mr. Corbett," and then turned toward Mr. Fry with a smug look and stated, "I have no further questions of this witness at this time."

Judge Crabtree advised Mr. Fry that the witness was ready to be crossed.

John Fry remained in his chair while he questioned Tom Corbett, "Mr. Corbett, after the incident with Mr. Zachariah, did Mr. Zachariah appear to be angry at what had just happened?"

Tom tilted his head and looked thoughtfully up at the ceiling and then looked at Mr. Fry, "No, he didn't appear to be angry at all, come to think about it."

Mr. Fry then asked, "Have you ever seen my client angry in any way?"

Tom Corbett stared into space a moment and then answered, "No, I don't believe I have ever seen him angry at anyone."

Mr. Fry looked through his notes briefly and then asked, "And is it your testimony here today that you were not with Zachariah on the one day that it rained here in Wheat awhile back, is that right?"

"That is right." Tom answered.

Mr. Fry leaned forward in his chair, "Do you know where Zachariah was on the day and time that it rained so hard, Mr. Corbett?"

"Yes," Tom Corbett replied. Tom Corbett's answer grabbed the attention of the entire room, especially that of Mr. Davis. He explained, "He was on my acreage out by the old Coleville place. We'd been working on my John Deere and I left him there while I drove on back home to go fetch us some dinner. When I got home it rained like a banshee. When I went back to check on Zachariah he was still working away, wet, but not complainin'."

Mr. Fry appeared as surprised as everyone else, "And what was my client wearing at that time?"

Tom Corbett didn't hesitate with his answer, "Bibs."

John Fry blinked hard. He was as confused as anyone else and ended his cross examination with a bewildered, "I have nothing further."

Richard W. Davis was worried that his case was falling apart. He was not about to let his reputation go to the birds either, especially now that there were reporters from four other newspapers from around the state in the building. It was time to play hardball. "Mr. Corbett, do you remember speaking to me in this very room yesterday afternoon about what your testimony would be today?" Davis demanded.

Tom Corbett could see that the prosecutor was less than pleased with him. "Yes," Tom answered innocently.

Mr. Davis reminded him, "You told me that you weren't with Zachariah when it rained on that day, isn't that what you told me just yesterday afternoon?"

Tom felt offended. He felt he had answered all the questions truthfully and specifically. He was a working man, a good man, and felt the city-slicker was trying to slight him in front of everyone. Tom Corbett replied in a way that let the prosecutor know that he was not going to be his whipping post. "You asked me if I was with Zachariah when it rained. I told you I wasn't and I wasn't. You never asked me where

Zachariah was, and if you had just asked, I would have told you."

Mr. Davis threw his head back and his arms outward and then slapped his hands back down at his sides. He then looked down at his highly polished Italian leather shoes and then back at Tom Corbett who had his chest stuck out ready for the next question. "How far away is your acreage out by… is it the old Coleville place, I dare to ask?" Davis inquired in a tone that sounded defeated.

Tom Corbett's answer was not what Mr. Davis was hoping to hear, but he expected it, "Five and a half miles north of town and to your left," Corbett replied.

"No further questions," Mr. Davis said as he shook his head and walked back to his chair.

John Fry was still staring out into space. All the witnesses seem to be telling the truth. They had no known reason to make up their stories. He turned and looked at Zachariah who smiled back at him. John Fry was beginning to wonder who this man was beside him. Things were getting very strange.

Four local witnesses testified on the second day of the trial. The first three had nothing helpful to say for either side. There was no doubt though that this quiet stranger was a mystery man, a very helpful mystery man at that.

Clara Swanson was the fourth and last witness to testify that afternoon. She made her way to the witness stand quickly after Sheriff Dan swore her in. Clara held her chin up and kept a small purse clutched on her lap. She was wearing a burgundy colored Cossack style pert hat, and a light blue floral printed dress with a high collar and a necklace with a small silver cross.

Judge Crabtree turned to the prosecutor, Mr. Davis, and Counsel John Fry and told them, "Let's move this along gentlemen." He was letting them know that he didn't want to go too far into the afternoon because once again it was getting very hot in the courtroom.

"Good morning Mrs. Swanson," Mr. Davis announced.

Clara responded respectfully, "Good morning sir."

"Could you tell the court where you reside, the address of where you live?" The prosecutor asked politely.

"I live at 501 Spring Road," Clara replied.

Mr. Davis slowly stood up behind his desk and tapped the end of his pencil on his notepad as he spoke, "So, you don't live too far from the Parsons Hardware & Feed, would that be right."

"About five blocks," Clara volunteered.

Mr. Davis waved his pencil in front of him and asked the next question, "And we're not talking big city blocks like in

New York or Chicago, we're talking much smaller blocks here, is that right Mrs. Swanson?"

Clara wasn't one to beat around the bush. "Well, certainly, all you have to do is look outside, Wheat is not a big city," she answered.

Mr. Davis walked to the side of his desk but kept his distance from the witness stand. After the testimony of the other witnesses he was a bit gun-shy and wasn't sure what might come out of Clara Swanson's mouth.

"Have you ever walked from your house to the Parsons Hardware & Feed, Mrs. Swanson?" the prosecutor inquired.

Clara answered without hesitation, "Oh, many times, many times."

At that moment Clara Swanson's testimony was interrupted when there was a distraction behind the gallery. Hazel Spragg had just entered the courtroom for the first time. She was completely dressed in black including long black gloves, a black hat with a black polk-a-dot veil and she had a folded handkerchief held up to her mouth. She looked as though she was in mourning as she made her way to a seat in the back row. Those who knew Hazel rolled their eyes without much pity for the woman who was trying to make her feelings known. Clara Swanson's chin dropped when she saw Hazel, because she knew Hazel was grieving over her loss of any hope of ever finding a man and was sympathetic to her plight.

Mr. Davis stared at Hazel for a moment wondering if there was something about the woman in black that he might have missed. He finally turned back to Clara Swanson, who was still staring at Hazel, and went back to work. "Mrs. Swanson," Mr. Davis went on, "how long does it take to walk from your house to Parsons Hardware & Feed?"

Clara thought about the question briefly and then replied, "That would depend on how fast you wanted to get there. I suppose if you were just walking normally it would take about...well...between five and ten minutes."

"Between five and ten minutes," Mr. Davis repeated loudly hoping that the jury was paying close attention. "And on the afternoon, early evening of Thursday, August 31st of this year, I understand you were with the defendant, Mr. Zachariah, at your home, is that true?"

Clara answered, "Yes, that is true."

Mr. Davis felt confident enough to come closer to the witness stand to ask the next question. "Was there a special occasion that evening why Mr. Zachariah would be at your house at that time?"

"He was helping me prepare dinner. He'd done some work for me and I decided to have him over for dinner with me, Betty Kinney and her children, and Hazel Spragg. There really was no special occasion. We were just getting together for some good Christian fellowship and after dinner we had planned to go play Bingo together, with Hazel and Betty that is. Thursday night is Bingo night around here."

Mr. Davis came a bit closer and seemed to be walking carefully as if he was concerned he might step on a landmine at anytime. "What time did your guests arrive that evening? Do you remember, Mrs. Swanson?"

Clara frowned briefly, "They never did. It rained so hard that it kept everyone home. The roads were a mess and we didn't get to have our ham dinner together and we couldn't go play Bingo."

"So you recall that it rained." Mr. Davis then asked her, "Where were you when it rained?"

Clara glanced over at Zachariah and then responded, "I was upstairs. I had gone up to my sewing room to look for some table linens. Then it started raining. It came down and was pounding on my roof. It came down so hard I thought my roof would fall in." Clara Swanson was leaning forward and was obviously amazed about the sudden rain.

"I see," Mr. Davis noted. "And where was Mr. Zachariah when it rained?" Mr. Davis was pointing to Zachariah when he asked the question. Zachariah sat quietly like always and looked like an innocent lamb ready to be slaughtered.

"He was downstairs in my kitchen peeling potatoes," Clara answered.

Mr. Davis smiled as if he had set his hook in a prize size trout at a fishing derby. "He was downstairs in your kitchen peeling potatoes," the prosecutor repeated loudly once again for the jury's sake. "And how do you know that, Mrs. Swanson?"

Clara Swanson looked directly into the prosecutor's eyes and replied, "Because I had been down there peeling carrots while he was peeling potatoes. We were cooking a big ham dinner with vegetables. I left him for a bit to go upstairs to look for my table linens. That is when it rained."

Mr. Davis walked over and faced the jury with a large smile. He looked into the eyes of each one of them trying to raise their suspicions and get their attention. Some of them were still trying to figure out who the woman in black was and how she fit in.

"Where was Mr. Zachariah when you came back down to the kitchen, Mrs. Swanson?"

Clara sat up in her chair and slowly lowered her chin. She was a woman who avoided the sin of lying, and certainly would not lie on the witness stand now. Yet, she had spent a lot of time with Zachariah and just couldn't imagine him having such a dark side. There was a long uncomfortable pause in the courtroom.

Suddenly in the back row of the gallery Hazel Spragg jumped up from her chair and with a loud pitiful moan cried out, "HE WAS WITH ME!" Hazel threw her arms over her eyes and

gave a horribly cheap Hollywood attempt at fainting and then
fell to the floor. Every newspaper reporter in the room got a
picture of the dramatic woman before she went down.

Judge Crabtree slammed his gavel down several times as
some of the men and ladies in the gallery went to Hazel's aid.
Judge Crabtree ordered the sheriff to go over and handle the
scene. Some of the women fanned Hazel who was still badly
faking her fainting spell. She was placed in a sitting position
as she pretended to come around. Sheriff Dan snagged her by
one of her arms and picked her up off the floor. Shaking his
head he escorted her out of the building with a trail of
sympathetic women following behind.

Judge Crabtree ordered a side-bar and had Mr. Davis and Mr.
Fry step up beside his bench. "What on earth was that all
about?" the judge demanded. Both Mr. Davis and Mr. Fry
looked sincerely bewildered and told him that they had no
idea. The judge scowled and in a not so quiet whisper said,
"Then someone had better find out. If she is a witness I want
to know about it and she had better not enter this courtroom
again unless she is on the witness stand, do you both
understand me?" Both Mr. Davis and Mr. Fry nodded their
heads in obedience and then looked suspiciously at each
other wondering if the other had set up the bizarre scene.

"Proceed Mr. Davis," the judge ordered.

"Yes, your Honor." Mr. Davis replied respectfully after the
judge's brow beating and continued his line of questions.
"Once again, Mrs. Swanson, you just testified that you were

in the kitchen peeling carrots while Mr. Zachariah was peeling potatoes and then you left him for a time to go upstairs to find table linens, is that the way it happened?"

Clara nodded her head, "That is the way it happened."

"What was Zachariah using to peel potatoes, Mrs. Swanson?" the prosecutor asked.

Clara looked down at her purse that was still in her lap to avoid eye contact with the prosecutor, "A paring knife…a small paring knife."

"A small paring knife!" Mr. Davis repeated again loudly making sure the jury was paying attention. John Fry rolled his eyes and sat back in his chair. "Tell me more about that paring knife, Mrs. Swanson. Was it sharp?"

Clara looked at Mr. Fry and then looked back at the prosecutor, "Yes, it was very sharp. It is my best paring knife."

Mr. Davis walked back and forth in front of his desk with his hand on his chin and then stopped quickly in front of the witness stand and turned toward Clara Swanson. It was as though he had rehearsed this move many times. "What was Mr. Zachariah wearing that evening?"

Clara looked over at Zachariah and then back at the prosecutor, "He was wearing the suit he is wearing now."

"Are you sure, Mrs. Swanson?" Mr. Davis tested her.

"Yes, I am sure," Clara replied, "he only has two pairs of clothes, that white suit and a pair of bib overalls that Hazel Spragg bought him. He was wearing one of my aprons while we were preparing dinner, though, and he didn't have his suit jacket on at the time, but he was wearing it when he came over."

"And was Zachariah still in the kitchen when you came back downstairs, Mrs. Swanson?" Mr. Davis asked.

Clara paused before answering, "No, he was gone."

The gallery in the courtroom became restless and noisy again as people began whispering to each other. "He was gone!" Mr. Davis shouted. "Where did he go, Mrs. Swanson?"

Clara answered quickly and a bit of frustration could be heard in her voice, "I don't know where he went."

"Did he ever come back that evening?" Mr. Davis asked quickly trying to keep the flow going his way.

"No, he never did," Clara answered.

"Did he ever tell you….strike that." Mr. Davis remembered that Zachariah could not talk…allegedly."Nothing further at this time, your Honor." Mr. Davis reported sounding pretty sure of himself.

Judge Crabtree turned to John Fry and let him know it was his turn to cross the witness.

"Hello, Mrs. Swanson," Mr. Fry said as he stood up and walked from behind the table. Mr. Fry's voice was unanimated and at a much lower volume than the prosecutor's. "Mrs. Swanson, what type of mood was Zachariah in when you last saw him on the evening of August 31st?"

Clara had settled back down and replied comfortably, "He was fine. I was singing songs and everything was just fine. He seemed very happy at the time."

"Have you ever seen Zachariah behave any way other than happy-go-lucky, Mrs. Swanson?"

Clara knew what Mr. Fry was trying to get her to say, "I have never seen this man angry. Oh, I suppose I have seen him appear deep in thought, but never angry. It's hard to say what he's thinking because he don't talk. But one thing I do know, is that I have never seen him mean to a soul and that is the gospel truth."

Mr. Fry then returned to his chair and stated, "Thank you, Mrs. Swanson, I have nothing…" Mr. Fry then looked on his notepad and then looked back up at the witness. "Oh, one more thing Mrs. Swanson, that paring knife, was it still in the kitchen when you went downstairs?"

Clara Swanson tilted her head to the side and was thinking to herself. She then lifted her chin high again and replied emphatically, "Yes, it was. The knife was still on the cutting board with the potatoes. Zachariah had finished peeling and cutting all the potatoes and the rest of my carrots too."

Mr. Davis winced in pain. He had intentionally left that question out and hoped it wouldn't come up. Once again Zachariah had dodged a bullet.

Judge Crabtree went to pour a glass of water from his pitcher, but the pitcher was empty. "Is this witness excused Mr. Davis?" Mr. Davis gave a defeated nod. "We'll be adjourning for the day, ladies and gentleman. Remember, no discussing this case. I don't want anyone of you talking to reporters and be back here at 7:30 a.m. tomorrow morning."

That evening Sheriff Dan walked back to the jail cell where Zachariah sat on his bunk staring at a blank wall. It had cooled off considerably and the sheriff had a thick fresh slice of chocolate cake that his wife made. Dan Devine was mystified by the quiet stranger. He was totally confused by the testimony that he heard and at the same time cautious. He had seen Ernie's throat and had heard about psychotic murderers in his day. But at the same time, he had been around Zachariah enough to know that there was surely something good about the man and every human being deserves the benefit of the doubt.

Sheriff Dan opened the cell and put the plate of cake on a small table beside Zachariah's bed. Zachariah smiled gratefully, picked up the plate and held it on his lap and stared thankfully at the sheriff. Sheriff Dan reached out across the open door to a desk in the hallway in front of the jail cell and pulled out a piece of paper and a pencil. He laid the paper down on the table and put the pencil on top of it.

"I don't know if you understand me, Zachariah. I don't know if you know what is going on at all, but if you can, I want you to write something on this piece of paper. If you can't write then draw me something, anything. I just need to know what is going on inside your head. We all do." The sheriff stared at Zachariah for a moment and walked out of the room and closed the cell door. "You're going to need a glass of milk with that. I'll go fetch it and then you need to eat that cake and get some sleep. You got a big day ahead of you."

Zachariah looked at the chocolate cake and then over at the paper and pencil on top of the table. He then, like Clara Swanson had testified, became deep in thought.

THE SURPRISE WITNESS
Chapter Twelve

It was 6:00 a.m. when Sheriff Dan Devine returned to the
Dixon County Building to get Zachariah ready for trial.
Zachariah was already dressed and sitting on the side of his
bed in his jail cell looking as though he was ready to go to a
church service. The glass of milk and the plate were now
empty. Sheriff Dan unlocked the cell and went over to the
small table next to the bed to fetch the glass and plate and
noticed the paper and pencil still on top of the table. The
sheriff had completely forgotten that he had left them for
Zachariah the night before. However, as he came close to the
table he realized that Zachariah had drawn something on the
paper. Sheriff Dan picked up the paper and stared at it. His
eyes opened wide in total awe. It was a beautifully drawn
picture of some type of angelic being standing with its wings
wide open on top of a mountain. There were doves in flight
and an ancient city below in the background. Dan Devine had
never seen such a beautiful and detailed drawing in his life.
The drawing looked as though it had been created by a
master artist.

Sheriff Dan looked closely at the amazing drawing and then
looked at Zachariah who was smiling at him. "Who are
you?" Sheriff Dan asked in true astonishment. Zachariah
looked at the sheriff with a kind expression as if he
understood the sheriff's confusion. Somehow, without saying

a word, Zachariah seem to be telling the sheriff that everything was going to be all right.

By 6:30 a.m., Main Street in the town of Wheat looked like a busy metropolis. There were automobiles with license plates from Missouri, Oklahoma, Arkansas, and Texas. A line had formed in front of Margie Kittles' Diner, mostly newspaper reporters with their press hats and cameras. The town was full of strangers, most of them curiosity seekers and reporters in a frenzy to learn more about the quiet mysterious stranger who was accused of a violent murderer.

A crowd of reporters had circled around Pete Barnes who was standing in front of Margie Kittles' place asking him questions, while inside, Margie was posing for the photographers. One of the reporters picked up a table knife and had Margie hold it in her hand to show the world what the murderer's knife that killed Ernie Parsons might have looked like. Wheat had become the mid-west's center of attention overnight. It went from a sleepy slow moving town to a busy circus side-show of pure chaos.

It didn't take long after the front doors of the courtroom were opened for the masses to begin pushing and shoving to get inside. They had to race for their seats before court commenced. The mob coming into the building was like a jammed funnel for a period of time. Every available seat was filled in less than five minutes and every square inch of standing room was taken. No less than fifty people stood outside the open front doors trying to get a glimpse of the trial, especially of the now infamous Zachariah. People "shooshed" each other as they strained to hear the testimony inside.

After Sheriff Dan Devine had settled the crowd down, Mr. Davis called him to the stand to testify. The sheriff walked towards the witness stand and stopped to face Judge Crabtree with a lost expression on his face. "Who's gonna swear me in?" the sheriff asked.

Judge Crabtree looked over his glasses and replied, "You are, you should know the lines by now."

Sheriff Dan looked puzzled. He removed his hat and raised his right hand and then began to swear himself in, talking very quickly, "I solemnly swear to tell the truth, the whole truth and nothin' but the truth….so help me…so help me…God." He then looked around the room, sort of embarrassed, and then sat down in the chair of the witness stand.

"Good morning Sheriff," Mr. Davis began.

"Howdy," the sheriff answered in a deep official tone.

"How long have you been sheriff in this county, Sheriff Devine?" the prosecutor inquired
.

"I was elected sheriff in 1925," the sheriff answered.

"And when did you see the defendant, Mr. Zachariah, for the first time?"

"On the day he first come into town, I saw him sitting in Margie Kittles' Diner not long after she opened that morning," the sheriff told him.

Mr. Davis sat and stared at his notepad for a moment and then stood up and leisurely walked over in front of the jury before he asked his next question. "And I understand that you found a man, Mr. Tom Kinney, dead at his filling station garage only hours prior, would that be right?"

John Fry rolled his eyes.

The Sheriff gave a big nod of agreement, "Yes, I did."

Mr. Davis went into his overacting prosecutor routine and put his fingers up on his forehead as if he was having difficulty figuring something out. "Now, let me make sure I get this straight. You found Tom Kinney dead inside his filling station garage which, if I am correct, is directly next to Margie Kittles' Diner, and a few hours later you see this stranger, this so called Zachariah for the first time in your town?"

John Fry had heard enough, "Objection, Mr. Davis is leading the witness and most of this has been asked and answered."

Judge Crabtree obviously disagreed, "Continue Mr. Davis."

The prosecutor walked back towards the witness stand and tried to insult Mr. Fry by grinning at him before turning back to the sheriff. "Sheriff, you responded to the Parsons Hardware & Feed on the afternoon, early evening, when the decedent Ernest Parsons was murdered did you not?"

"Yes, I did, I got a call from Ruthie McCabe who got a call from Ernie's wife, Millie. Millie was hysterical and I couldn't tell what Millie was saying so I went on over and....found Ernie."

Mr. Davis came close to the sheriff and folded his arms. "Describe to the court, Sheriff Devine, what you found, and in full detail if you will."

The sheriff raised his eyebrows and took a deep breath. It was obvious that he didn't want to discuss the grizzly details in mixed company, there were ladies in the audience and even some young ears outside listening in. He tapped on his knees and then reluctantly and slowly began telling his story. "Well, I actually ran over to the Hardware & Feed from my office that's here in this building. It had just rained something fierce and the roads were full of standing water and mud. Strange thing having that rain all of a sudden and then it was gone in a flash. Anyway, Millie was still inside the building, I could hear her crying and moaning. I found Ernie Parsons lying on his back in the mud just outside of the front porch. His arms were spread out from his side, his mouth and eyes were still open, but he was dead. His throat had been slit clean open."

The sound and the bright lights of camera flashbulbs lit up the courtroom. The news reporters excitedly wrote down their version of the sheriff's description of finding the body of Ernie Parsons. Some of the reporters rushed out of the courtroom to hunt down telephones to call their newsrooms. The murder trial in Wheat was front page news that couldn't wait.

Mr. Davis was on top of the world, or so he thought. He got the attention of the jurors by making eye contact with them before asking the next question. "Did your investigation lead to the arrest of the defendant, Mr. Zachariah, Sheriff Devine?"

Sheriff Devine nodded his head and replied, "Yes it did."

No further questions at this time, your Honor," the prosecutor concluded.

"Your cross," Judge Crabtree told Mr. Fry.

Mr. Fry stood up and took a seat again at the corner of the counsel table. "Sheriff Devine, you've heard the testimony of the witnesses in this trial and you conducted your own investigation into the death of Ernest Parsons, is that correct?"

The sheriff agreed, "Yes, that is right."

"So how many people have told you that they saw my client, Mr. Zachariah, murder Mr. Parsons?"

"One person," was the simple answer provided by the sheriff.

"And shortly after leaving the terrible incident at the Parsons Hardware & Feed you went directly over to where Mr. Zachariah was residing and arrested him, did you not?" Mr. Fry asked firmly.

"I did," the sheriff answered.

Mr. Fry walked over to the jury and ran his hand down the front wooden rail as the prosecutor had done a couple days earlier, "What was Mr. Zachariah wearing when you arrested him?"

Sheriff Dan looked over at Mr. Fry and answered, "His pair of bib overalls that Hazel Spragg had bought him. He had on a white work shirt underneath and a pair of old work boots that Skinny Jim Carter gave him some time ago."

"Was Mr. Zachariah wet? Was he wet at all sheriff?" The sheriff looked baffled as he recalled the day he arrested Zachariah.

"No, not wet at all and his white suit was hung up by his bed, clean and dry. His shoes and his boots didn't have any mud on them and I didn't find any knife in his little place."

Mr. Fry looked shamefully at the sheriff and his tone matched his expression, "I am confused, Sheriff Devine, what facts did you have to arrest Zachariah for a serious crime such as....*Murder*?"

The sheriff felt like crawling under a rock, but in his mind at the time of the arrest, he thought he had made the right decision. But now he was worried that he may have been very wrong.

Sometimes a lawman has to make difficult choices based on how believable a person is…or seemed to be at the time. The sheriff tried to explain his decision to arrest Zachariah. "Millie Parsons is one of the most level headed, respectful, honest people in this town. I have known her since she was a young girl and I have never known her to make up a story. She's a kind hearted woman and would never cause a lick of trouble to no one. Millie Parsons is a person you can trust and I believed her when she told me what she saw. That was good enough for me."

Sheriff Devine's confidence in his decision to arrest Zachariah grew stronger as he spoke. He had convinced himself, possibly the only one in the courtroom anyway, that he had made the right decision.

"Thank you sheriff," Mr. Fry told him. "Your Honor, I have no further questions for this witness."

Judge Crabtree ordered a 15 minute break to allow for the rear doors to be opened to get fresh air into the stuffy room. It was only 8:30 in the morning and was already like an oven in the courtroom. It was going to be another scorcher in Wheat.

Other than the judge and Mr. Davis, no one left the courtroom. Floor space was in high demand and no one inside was willing to give up their precious spot for anything. When it was about time to reconvene, Sheriff Devine walked up to Mr. Fry and told him he was needed in the judge's chambers.

In the judges' makeshift chambers, Judge Crabtree explained to Mr. Fry that a new witness would be testifying for the state.

John Fry was concerned, "I haven't been told about this witness, who is it and what are they suppose to testify to?"

Mr. Davis attempted to answer the question, "She's a woman from up near Kansas City. She can identify your client from an automobile accident up by Valley Falls a few years back."

Mr. Fry was not going to allow this surprise witness to testify. "So what does she know about my client that you believe has any relevance to this trial? You can't just throw a witness up on that stand without going through due process. How do we know she's credible? She could be just another one of these other screwballs that read about this trial and is looking to get her picture in the paper. I'm not going to allow it."

Judge Crabtree interrupted Mr. Fry's valiant plea however, it was the judge's show. "Mr. Fry, do I need to remind you that I'm the only one here wearing a black robe. I am going to allow this witness to testify today. She is a cripple and has gone through great pains to be here today. Mr. Davis tells me that this woman can positively identify your client and will testify that this Mr. Zachariah fellow can actually speak. She will be allowed to testify Mr. Fry, but I will limit her testimony to that question only Mr. Davis." The judge continued the conversation with other court matters. "How many more witnesses do you two have?"

The prosecutor spoke first, "After Mrs. Rayburne, I just have Millie Parsons and she won't take long. However, I do have a request Judge Crabtree. I would like to take the jury out to the scene of the crime, out to Parsons Hardware & Feed. I believe they need to see where this all began and to be able to see for themselves the distances between some of the locations the witnesses have been talking about."

Judge Crabtree looked over at John Fry anticipating a strong argument. Mr. Fry wasn't going to bother and said sarcastically, "I suppose I could object to that, but at this point I doubt if anyone cares." Mr. Fry was right. The judge turned back to Mr. Davis, "And how do you think we could pull this off with half the state of Kansas here in this town, Mr. Davis?"

The prosecutor had already thought the problem through. "Have the sheriff rope off the streets around the Hardware & Feed and conduct a lottery for the reporters. We could limit the reporters to say…three and you could warn the rest of the crowd that they'll be arrested or at least fined if they come inside the roped off area."

Judge Crabtree bought Mr. Davis' proposal but allowed a total of five reporters to join the court at Parsons Hardware & Feed. He wanted to get the most out of his trial's press coverage as possible without making it obvious. "And what time shall we have this testimony at the Parsons?" the judge inquired.

John Fry turned to Mr. Davis knowing he'd already have an answer. After all, it had become Mr. Davis' trial. "The sheriff needs time to set up the restricted area around the Parsons' place, so let's make it 5:30 p.m."

John Fry wasn't surprised. It was determined that Ernie Parsons had died at about that time and the counselor knew that the prosecutor was only trying to get as much shock value as he could. Mr. Fry closed his eyes in frustration and only shook his head to give his answer.

"Very well then," Judge Crabtree agreed, "we can close this up first thing tomorrow morning."

A HOSTILE WITNESS
Chapter Thirteen

John Fry's chair was pulled back from the table as he sat low with legs stretched out and doodled on his notepad. Zachariah looked over his attorney's shoulder and curiously looked at the drawings. Suddenly, there were sounds of shuffling and murmurs from the gallery as Virginia Rayburne made her way through the crowd to the witness stand. Her assistant, Tess, pushed Mrs. Rayburne in her wheelchair. Tess, a homely plump woman frowned at the probing spectators as they gawked at the woman in the wheelchair as they tried to get a glimpse of her face.

Mrs. Rayburne's legs were covered with a black and silver colored silk blanket. She was wearing a matching colored silk dress with long sleeves and black silk gloves. She also wore a panama style hat that was tilted on her head and a dark veil that fully covered her face. From the jeweled necklace and bracelets the woman was wearing there was no doubt that she was certainly not from Wheat. All eyes closely followed Mrs. Rayburne as she made her way to the front of the courtroom where she was turned around to face the gallery in front of the witness stand. Her assistant, Tess, straightened out her blanket and then moved a short distance to the side where she could keep a watchful eye on her employer.

Mr. Davis put on his choir boy face and approached Mrs. Rayburne, "Good morning, Mrs. Rayburne."

Mrs. Rayburne kept her face down and remained very still and quiet. Finally she answered in a soft voice that was nearly inaudible, "Good morning."

Mrs. Rayburne had not been out in public since her accident. She occasionally looked up at the people in the courtroom, peeping through her veil. She looked like a frightened deer crouched helplessly in front of a pack of lions.

"Mrs. Rayburne," Mr. Davis asked very kindly, "could you tell the court where you are from?"

Remaining perfectly still the woman replied, "Bonner Springs."

Mr. Davis walked up beside Mrs. Rayburne making sure he didn't block her view from the jurors. "Bonner Springs, my, that is a good distance from Wheat," the prosecutor commented. "Do you see anyone in this room that looks familiar?"

The woman remained frozen in her wheelchair for an uncomfortably long time but finally raised her right hand and pointed a finger at Zachariah.

Mr. Davis looked pleased. "Let it be known that Mrs. Rayburne pointed to the defendant who is known only to the court as Mr. Zachariah." Mr. Davis bent over and continued to speak softly to the woman, "Do you know that man's name, Mrs. Rayburne?"

Mrs. Rayburne shook her head slowly to state that she did not know the man's name.

"You don't know his name," Mr. Davis answered for her. "Then if you would, Mrs. Rayburne, could you tell the court how you know the defendant and what you know about him. And please Ma'am, we will need you to speak up a little so that the jurors can hear your voice."

John Fry sat up in his chair and leaned forward and was very anxious to hear what the response would be.

Mrs. Rayburne remained motionless for a moment. Finally, she cleared her voice and began to speak. At first her voice seemed frail but it became stronger and louder as she spoke. "In the summer of 1928 my husband, Chester, and I decided to take a drive out to Lake Perry to spend the day together. It was the first anniversary of our wedding and it was a nice warm day. We were on Highway 4 near Valley Falls when we saw...that man there walking alongside the road out in nowhere. He was wearing that same white suit and looked exactly the same as he does today. My husband told me that he wanted to give the man a lift but I told him it wasn't a good idea. There are always plenty of unruly drifters and vagabonds along the highways and bi-ways. I urged my husband not to, but Chester had a kind and trusting heart and didn't pay me any attention. It was the biggest mistake of his life. We pulled over and Chester told the man to hop in the back of our truck, we had a new 1928 Chevrolet at the time. I'm not totally sure how long it was after we picked up the stranger, but a deer suddenly ran out in front of our truck and Chester got startled. He turned the stirring wheel hard to avoid hitting the creature and we struck a large tree off the side of the road. Before I knew what happened I was lying on the ground with the truck lying on top of me on its side. Gasoline was pouring out on the ground and getting all over me. My body was crushed and I couldn't move. Somehow there was fire and I started burning alive. I screamed for my husband but he never answered. Then I looked up and saw him lying in the middle of the street. He'd been thrown out of the truck after we hit that tree. He wasn't moving. Then I saw… that man, that Zachariah man, bend down over my husband and say something into his ear. I couldn't hear what he was saying but he was saying something. That's all that I remember. I never saw him again until yesterday when I saw his picture in the newspaper. I would never forget his face in a thousand years."

Mr. Davis listened intently at the woman's sad story and seemed to be genuinely moved by the pain that she had suffered. "Mrs. Rayburne, I am so sorry that you had to suffer such grievous pain and for the loss of your beloved husband. But do you have any…proof that it was Mr. Zachariah that you saw on that tragic day in the summer of 1928?"

Before anyone could prepare themselves for the shock, Mrs. Rayburne quickly pulled off her veiled hat to reveal her hideously burned face. One of her eyes was melted closed and on the same side of her head, her ear had been burned away and she had only a few strands of hair remaining. Her dreadful appearance caused a loud repulsive response from the crowd in the courtroom.

Virginia Rayburne's voice rang out loudly and angrily in the courtroom, "This is your *proof*, Mr. Davis. This is what happens when the *Angel of Death* walks into your path. That man is the murdering son of Satan himself." Mrs. Rayburne stared furiously at Zachariah who remained calm as usual but looked somewhat puzzled. "I shall never forget his face," Mrs. Rayburne began to sob, "Never!"

Judge Crabtree struck his gavel several times to get the gallery to settle and quiet down and to put an end to Mrs. Rayburne's testimony. Mr. Davis was too shocked to respond. Mrs. Rayburne's assistant went over to Mrs. Rayburne, who now had crumbled into tears, and put her hat back on and comforted her. The gallery was relieved that the woman's head and face were once again hidden from view, yet still some were a bit disturbed by the shocking scene.

The judge asked Mr. Fry if he wanted to cross examine Mrs. Rayburne, but asked it in a way that he was hoping he wouldn't.

Mr. Fry stood up and walked up in front of Mrs. Rayburne and he appeared to be thinking deeply, "Mrs. Rayburne was there anyone else around at the time of this horrible accident. I mean, besides you, your husband and…Mr. Zachariah?"

Mrs. Rayburne shook her head and replied while trying to control her crying, "No, it was just the three of us."

Mr. Fry pressed on, "And you were pinned underneath the truck when you saw your husband, Chester, in the street and…you were burning, is that right?"

Mrs. Rayburne nodded again slowly and replied, "Yes, of course, I thought I made that obvious."

Mr. Fry tilted his head and thought again for a moment trying to picture in his mind the scene of the horrible accident. "What happened next?" he asked her.

Mrs. Rayburne took in a slow breath and then answered with a soft voice, "I don't know. I woke up and I was lying next to a tree a ways off. Eventually, some people traveling along the highway stopped and helped me, drove me to the hospital."

Mr. Fry pulled in his chin and tried to see the woman's face through her veil, "And what happened to Mr. Zachariah?"

Mrs. Rayburne looked into Mr. Fry's eyes and replied, "I don't know, I never saw him again in person until today."

Mr. Fry walked back towards his chair looking at Zachariah and commented under his breath, "Interesting. I have nothing further."

People in the gallery whispered to one another and the reporters furiously finished taking their notes. The judge announced that the court would be recessing until 5:00 p.m. and that if any reporters were interested they would have to take part in a drawing from a hat to attend the testimony of the final witness. After he explained the afternoon procedures the judge warned the crowd, "And let me make myself perfectly clear, anyone crossing the rope barriers near the Parsons Hardware & Feed will be arrested for obstruction, and that goes for every man, woman or child. The rest of you can come back tomorrow morning for closing arguments. This court is in recess." The judge struck the gavel and the mass of reporters made their way towards Sheriff Devine to hopefully win their precious ticket in the courtroom lottery.

The trial in the little town of Wheat in the mostly unknown county of Dixon had become the biggest media frenzy in anyone's recollection. For three days in 1933 the boring rural town of Wheat was the center of the world.

THE KILLER IS REVEALED
Chapter Fourteen

At 5:15 p.m. Judge Crabtree began leading the parade of jurors threw a large crowd that had gathered on Main Street. The procession began at the Dixon County Building and went all the way to Parsons Hardware & Feed four blocks away. Some of the local men, including Pete Barnes, Ed Morlan, Skinny Jim Carter, Ray Horne, and Tom Corbett helped move the crowd back so that the convoy of court people could make their way to the crime scene. The prosecutor, Mr. Davis, followed behind the jurors while Mr. Fry walked closely after him. Directly behind Mr. Fry was Zachariah, with his wrists handcuffed in front and Sheriff Dan Devine leading him by the arm.

The onlookers struggled to get closer to see the event as if they were fan-crazed celebrity seekers. When Zachariah appeared, some of them waved at him trying to get his attention while others stared at him as if he was the devil himself incarnate.

As the group passed the rope barricades and approached the Hardware & Feed, Millie Parsons came out onto the porch. She was wearing a simple blue and green plaid dress that she usually wore and she looked very distraught. When she saw Zachariah she reeled her shoulders back slightly and stared at him with a mixture of anger and fear.

Judge Crabtree had the jurors stand in a half circle in front of the front porch of the hardware & feed and told the sheriff to swear Millie Parsons in. The sheriff stepped up onto the porch and walked up to Millie who was standing just outside of the business's front doors.

"Hello, Millie," the sheriff said kindly.

Millie nodded her head and greeted her friend, Dan Devine. "Millie would you please raise your right hand; do you Millie Parsons swear to tell the truth, the whole truth, nothing but the truth, so help you, God?"

Millie looked at the judge and answered sternly, "Yes, I certainly do."

Mr. Davis walked up on the front porch and began his questioning, "Mrs. Parsons, I know this is going to be extremely difficult to do, but would you tell the court what happened on the day that your husband was killed?"

Millie looked at the row of jurors standing in front of her and tried to find a friendly face she could concentrate on. She wasn't use to standing up in public and talking. She rubbed her hands together nervously and began to tell her story. "Well…my husband and I were inside the store, I guess it was about 5:30 p.m. or so, we were putting some things away and getting ready to close up. It started raining. It started raining very hard. The clouds came out of nowhere and at first we didn't know what it was because the rain drops hit the roof and the ground so hard. Ernie remembered that there were some sacks of grain out in front of the porch so he went outside to bring them in. I went to the storage closet to get Ernie's raincoat to put on so I could help him move goods out of the rain. When I got to the front door I saw him lying in the street...." Millie had held herself together fairly well until this point and then began to fall apart and cry.

The heartbroken woman became too emotional to carry on so Mr. Davis tried to distract her by helping her explain what she had witnessed. "So, Mrs. Parsons, the sacks of grain I am assuming were down here in front of the porch, is that right?"

Tears were streaming down Millie's face and she covered her mouth with one of her hands trying to control her crying. She was able to nod to let Mr. Davis know that he was correct.

"All right then," Mr. Davis continued as he walked off the porch in the area where Ernie would have gone to fetch the grain. The prosecutor was about ready to ask Millie Parsons another question when he noticed some of the jurors were distracted and looking around. It was beginning to rain.

There are some that say that lightning never strikes twice in the same place. However, that saying is certainly not true, at least it wasn't the case in the little town of Wheat in 1933. The following account of what happened next was recorded into the law books and witnessed by at least one hundred people, so it is without a doubt the absolute truth.

Although there was no wind to speak of, a group of rain clouds moved above the Parsons Hardware & Feed where the trial of the State of Kansas vs. John Doe Zachariah was taking place. It was the first time it had rained in Dixon County since the afternoon, early evening, of August 31st. The rain came so hard and fast that if one couldn't find a roof to hide under real quick, they got soaked.

Judge Crabtree and Mr. Fry along with the thirteen jurors jumped up onto the porch to avoid getting wet while the prosecutor, Mr. Davis, stood directly in front of the porch looking up in the sky. He was baffled. There had not been one cloud in the sky only a few seconds earlier. Sheriff Dan and Zachariah stood nearby as the rain proceeded to come down. The sheriff was also amazed as he looked around and watched the crowd scattering for cover. Zachariah stood still and looked as if he was being entertained while the rain dripped down from his hair and ran down his face.

"My word," the prosecutor said aloud as the rain came pouring down.

Call it destiny or call it fate, but all things work together in strange ways. If Sheriff Dan's careful investigation of what occurred next is correct then the truth be known. Why it happened is another thing.

Ernie Parsons had been a fairly good salesman, a good husband, sort of a good friend, but he hadn't been a good carpenter. He never was a patient man so he rushed the tasks of working on things like his truck and his tractor and such. Fixing or building anything correctly was not Ernie Parsons' calling.

Rain hitting the peak of the roof and running down the metal roofing was supposed to be captured by the new gutter system that Ernie Parsons had designed and built himself, which it did. But in his haste, Ernie did not attach downspouts to the rain troughs and with the great volume of rain that came down, the water built up quickly and had no place to go. There was a slight overhang above the front porch where a six foot piece of the sheet metal trough was attached to other sections of the gutter system. On one end of the trough Ernie hadn't nailed it sufficiently to the fascia and when it got full of heavy water it unattached from the fascia and came down with a good amount of force. With a razor sharp piece of sheet metal protruding at its end, the trough swung down like a deadly pendulum, emptying it's water along the way and making a full circle back to its original position.

Of course all of this was unknown at the present time. Mr. Davis was standing close to the same spot that Ernie Parsons had been standing and he was looking up towards the raining heavens as Ernie had been when poor Ernie met his fate. The rain trough once again was as full as it could get and down it came. "Swoooosh!"

It was just a simple flash before his eyes, but Mr. Davis knew that something had transpired. So did those who were watching. They looked dazed as they stood with their mouths hanging open and their eyes bulging. "Clunk," came the sound of the trough as it swung full circle back into its place.

And before you could say, "Sweet Jesus," the rain stopped and the clouds moved on their way.

Mr. Davis's wet hair was plastered to his head. He looked forward into nothingness and then looked down at the ground in front of his shoes where the severed remains of his necktie lay in the mud. He stepped back carefully and didn't say a word but looked as though he had just seen a ghost. No one said a word, they just stood there looking at the soggy and bewildered prosecutor. Sheriff Dan looked at Zachariah who looked back at him with an innocent smile. It was the weirdest thing anyone had ever witnessed.

ON THE ROAD AGAIN
Chapter Fifteen

One morning Skinny Jim Carter went out to check on
Zachariah who hadn't been seen since his release.
Zachariah's bib overalls that Hazel Spragg had bought him
were neatly folded and lying on his bed. The boots Skinny
Jim gave him were placed neatly on the floor at the foot of
the bed, but Zachariah was gone. The quiet stranger had left
Wheat as mysteriously as he had arrived.

It was the very next day, about 6:00 p.m. when Henry
Coyote's dogs became excited and started barking. Henry
was inside preparing to cook a rabbit that he had just shot and
skinned. As Henry walked to the open front door he looked
out and saw a stranger standing on the dirt road in front of his
house looking at him. It was Zachariah. Henry was halfway
expecting him.

The dogs were fiercely barking at the stranger but staying
back and not protecting their territory as if they were very
afraid of him. Henry Coyote stood and stared at Zachariah
for a moment and then motioned him with his hand to come
forward. As Zachariah walked towards the front door,
Henry's dogs began to back away and as the stranger came
closer they ran off behind the house like frightened puppies.

Zachariah stood just outside the front porch. "I have heard
about you, stranger." Henry said. "You have come a long
way. You must be thirsty." Henry motioned the stranger with

his head and Zachariah followed him inside. The house wasn't much more than a shack, but it was clean. Henry's grandfather sat inside near a fireplace and followed Zachariah closely with blind eyes that hadn't seen for many years. "This is my grandpa-Joe, Joe Pah-hu-ska," Henry told him, "he told me you were coming."

Zachariah looked at the old man. His leathery brown skin was full of years and his eyes were cloudy white with age. The two men's eyes stayed on each other as they sat in silence for quite some time. Finally, Joe Pah-hu-ska began speaking in his native tongue and Henry translated. "My grandfather said that you have traveled very far. The ravens told him that you were coming to sing your night song. Tsi-Shu, the Sky People, have come before but he will not listen. He will cover his ears and not listen to the messengers."

Zachariah stood looking at the old man as if he could understand every word he was saying even before Henry translated it. When Joe Pah-hu-ska was finished talking Zachariah lightly nodded his head and gave an understanding smile.

Henry handed Zachariah a tin cup of water, which he drank, and then handed the empty cup back to him. Zachariah smiled once more, turned around and walked out. He never returned to Henry Coyote's house again.

After the trial, Bingo games were the only event that brought people into Wheat, and all of those folks were more or less locals. Clara Swanson eventually moved away to live with her sister in Topeka and taught Sunday school at one of the Presbyterian churches. Ed Morlan's sight became so bad that he moved in with his son in Ohio. Margie Kittles married a traveling salesman and left everything she had including her diner behind with food still in the icebox. Pete Barnes suffered a heart attack and died about six months after the big murder trial in Wheat. Millie moved on and remarried a nice man who owned a feed store down in Independence. Big Tom Kinney's wife and kids moved up to Wichita and moved in with family. Nobody knows what happened to Hazel Spragg. Some say that she headed down to Mexico and married up with a rich governor from some city down there and had a bunch of kids. Others say that she never left her big house and drank her lonely self to death. Years later teenagers broke out all the windows of the old Spragg mansion and it was rumored for a time that Hazel's ghost could sometimes be heard moaning for her lost love at midnight.

Either way the entire town of Wheat dried up and blew away like a tumble-weed. Highway construction on US Route 75 probably didn't help any, but every town has its own lifespan. There are plenty of lost civilizations that would attest to that. Wheat was and is no more. It is only in the memories of the few that once passed through it and care to remember it.

Many miles away on a long straight highway surrounded by miles and miles of corn fields, an old farmer was making his way to town in his flat bed truck. He had several bales of hay and a few crates of chickens in the back to deliver to a marketplace. Up ahead, a lone traveler was walking alongside the highway going in the same direction. The farmer pulled over to the side of the road and offered the stranger a ride. The man looked harmless enough wearing his white cotton suit with a blue and red silk tie.

The traveler was happy to catch a ride and jumped up into the back of the truck where he made himself comfortable by leaning back between a couple bales of soft hay. With one of his arms folded behind his head Zachariah reached out with his other hand and pulled out a piece of straw to chew on. As he looked up into the big blue sky he smiled as he thought to himself - it was after all a beautiful day.

The End

www.ingramcontent.com/pod-product-compliance
Lightning Source LLC
Chambersburg PA
CBHW021116130626

46554CB00002B/725

9780985303013